# Let's Hear It for a Beautiful Guy

# Let's Hear It for a Beautiful Guy

### And Other Works of Short Fiction

## Bruce Jay Friedman

## DONALD I. FINE, INC.

*New York*

"An Ironic Yetta Montana" originally appeared in
Rolling Stone Magazine.
"The Mourner" and "The Adventurer" originally appeared in
Playboy Magazine.
"The Car Lover," "The Scientist," "A Different
Ball Game," and "The Pledges" originally
appeared in Esquire Magazine.
"Let's Hear It for a Beautiful Guy" originally
appeared in The New Yorker Magazine.
"Our Lady of the Lockers" originally appeared
in New York Magazine.
"The Best We Have" originally appeared in Gallery
Magazine.
"Marching Through Delaware" originally appeared
in Cosmopolitan Magazine.

*For Pat and Molly—with love*

# Contents

There is a story behind most stories and these are no exception. One of them ("Detroit Abe") represents the first part of a novel I never completed. Rust Hills of Esquire said I didn't go on with the book because I finished it in the first twenty-five pages and maybe he's right.

I wrote some of the stories quickly and took two years on one of them ("The Candide of Copiers"). If it succeeds, it's because I took out the allegedly best line. I found one of the stories ("Business is Business") in a trunk. An actual writer's trunk. It was written by a twenty-six-year-old fellow who happened to be me. Kid had some nice moves. In it went, as is.

One of the stories ("The Car Lover") was written as a play. No complex explanation. Two characters, one "set." It felt comfortable that way. Another, longer, ("Our Lady of the Lockers"), a deductive mystery, was written on "assignment." Very scary, writing fiction on assignment.

Many of the stories were written in the '60s and '70s; it would be nice to report that they reverberate with the turbulence of the times. What they seem to reverberate with is the fact that I was able to do them. I did not "update" them, changing "girl" to "woman," for example, but in each case have noted the year in which they were written.

Every Saturday afternoon, as an eight-year-old at Cejwin Camp, I sat at the lakeside and listened to the director, Dr. Schoolman, recite a story about the Wise Man of Chelm. I loved those once-upon-a-time stories, and yet I don't think I've ever written anything in the same spirit. Who leads a cozy once-upon-a-time life?

It was my publisher's idea that I write this introductory note. This means taking off the mask—but not necessarily. Think of this as a story about a fellow introducing his own stories.

—Bruce Jay Friedman
Water Mill, New York

# The Candide
# of Copiers

**F**IVE YEARS BEFORE, WHEN RAMIREZ left Alvin Kornfeld's office, he was—if not a new man—at least a more relaxed fellow at the plate. Cured? Lived there a man who could properly define that word? He still feared death and disabling injury. But what was he supposed to do, look forward to that combo? Perhaps there was a breed of psychiatrist who sent his charges whirling off to infinity with a song in their hearts. If such a man existed, Ramirez could not have cared less. Kornfeld had done a fine job. It would be virtually impossible to confuse Ramirez with the shambles of a man who had first shown up in the doctor's office with an ear hanging loose, the result of a reckless lunge at his ex-wife's station wagon. (At the wheel of the moving vehicle was a fly-by-night commodities broker whose design, consummated, as it happens, was to whisk Rebecca Ramirez off for a ten-day jaunt to a freshly-opened Club Med.) To top it all off, JoJo Ramirez, a ten-year-old son, lay hollow-eyed and manacled at a suburban police station, on a peeping charge. Slowly, over a five-year period, with a nudge here and a shove there, Kornfeld had helped Ramirez to stand erectly. If his back wasn't completely straight, at least he no longer hunched through life with an arm thrown up, as if to ward off blows.

To the best of his knowledge, it had been Ramirez's decision to call a halt to the treatment. One day he was off the couch, the next he was out the door. Or so he recalled it. But he was curious to know the ground rules. What if, one day, he fell victim to a mysterious cloud of gloom? Could he pop around for a quick visit? Or give Kornfeld a jingle on the phone? In the doctor's view, the best approach was over-and-out.

"How about a year-end check-up?" Ramirez was pleased

13

that he could ask this question with genuine curiosity—not, for a change, with a pounding heart.

"I don't think so," said Kornfeld.

"So this is it," said Ramirez, taking what he felt was a last look at Kornfeld's Mexican artifacts.

Surprisingly, it was the doctor's eyes that were the first to get wet.

"This is it," said Ramirez.

Without question, the moment was a powerful one, yet Ramirez chose to treat it with glibness. Perhaps this was reason alone for him to log another year of treatment—but he had decided to get going.

"Doc," he said, extending his hand. "It's been a helluva psychoanalysis." With a strange fumbling embrace, somewhere between a hug and a handshake, the two men said good-bye.

Virtually the moment he left Kornfeld's office, Ramirez—as far as his life was concerned—ran into a long smooth stretch of highway. Whether this was due to the doctor's ministrations or a hearty shove from Dame Fortune was anybody's guess. Playing no small part in the scenario was Lucy Greenhouse, the new woman in his life, who had appeared to him miraculously as a part-time cleaning lady, then stuck around to brighten up not only his furniture but his life as well. And she didn't stop cleaning either.

In his work, too, Ramirez prospered. As a designer of low-cost copying machines, he had always enjoyed a small cult following. And though he had never been able to draw a clean breath in the dollar department, his fees had enabled him, uneasily, to keep the wolf away from the door. Then, suddenly, as a result of what he considered a lackluster effort, his career took off. Unlike most copiers which had to work up a head of steam before they got going, the Ramirez 990 hit the ground copying. Nor did its assembly call for the traditional army of workers. Provided they all pulled together in the same direction, a small lighthearted team could slap one together in no time at all. Of all people, the Japanese—perhaps bored by too much sleekness and efficiency—were taken with its homespun slapdash makeup and ordered a ton of them. For the first time in his life, Ramirez had not only designed a copier but kept a piece of the action. Suddenly, he was showered with prosperity, although it was important to keep in mind that in the fast-breaking copier field (someone always copied your copier) success might be short-lived. Nonetheless, Ramirez enjoyed his good fortune. He bought a home in the Maine woods. There he worked on some amusing software for the 990 and fiddled with a "sequel" to his unexpected blockbuster. A prominent newsweekly featured his photograph in the business section with the caption: "The Ramirez 990—Flash-in-the-Pan or First Legitimate Thorn in IBM's Side?"

Thus, in his life, and in his all-important occupation, Ramirez flourished, although, predictably, it was not one hundred percent smooth sailing. Lucy Greenhouse was unquestionably the finest woman he had ever known. Yet, preposterously, he slipped off on occasion to highway motels, there to deaden his brain with drugs and hookers. When supplies of both ran out, and he was ready to howl through the window in frustration, he had often thought of calling Kornfeld, at least for a little Valium—but he held back because of embarrassment. In more controllable situations—a venomous call from his ex-wife, a spasm of hatred for his own child—Ramirez found that with a snap of his fingers he could summon up Kornfeld—a psychiatric genie—who, for the most part, would reinforce Ramirez's own judgment with a meaningful glance.

One day—not quite out of the blue, since Kornfeld had obviously seen his photograph in the noted newsweekly—

he received a letter from the doctor, congratulating him on his success and suggesting that it was the "humanity" of the Ramirez 990 that enabled it not only to survive but to stand out among the giants. "Take this away and it would be nothing," wrote Kornfeld, perhaps a bit harshly. Then, with self-deprecation, Kornfeld said he had gone to see the copier at a trade exhibition and actually enjoyed being shouldered aside in the crush of curiosity-seekers, all anxious to see the handiwork of his old friend. And he had changed his mind about his strict policy on get-togethers.

"I am not ashamed to say that I miss you, Hector," wrote Kornfeld. "And I would love to see you for a little lunch."

The letter confused Ramirez and put him on his guard. Kornfeld had written him on the occasion of a triumph. Where was he when Ramirez was howling out of motel windows for support? The doctor could not have known about his state, of course—yet, idiotically, his lack of concern rankled. Was it really Ramirez the individual he missed or Ramirez the celebrity? Then, too, what if Ramirez asked him a question or two about drugs and hookers? Would the lunch then constitute a session? Ramirez, of course, would be delighted to pay for it as such, but he didn't want to haggle about it in a roadside restaurant, which he was sure would have dark red leather booths and feature sliced beefsteak. But these were petty concerns. After all, it was Kornfeld he was speculating about—a man who had led him safely through darkness. He owed him this lunch. So he wrote back and said he would be thrilled to get together with him and would be in touch presently about the arrangements. Except that "presently" never seemed to arrive. He sent the doctor postcards from Paris and Tokyo—where the designer of the Ramirez 990 was given a rousing reception—but upon his return from the Far East, back he went to the woods. The Kornfeld lunch remained a modestly annoying pebble in his shoe. There was, perhaps, an easy explanation for the unconsummated reunion. Kornfeld dropped grenades. Why should Ramirez allow his life, which he was almost sure was satisfying, to be disturbed.

Predictably, in the normal course of events, it was disturbed anyway. One night, Ramirez, who had been drinking heavily at home, dropped into a local bar and found himself on the receiving end of an ethnic slur. Instead of registering his disgust and leaving, Ramirez stuck around—fending with his antagonist for hours. When the unlikely offender—a sociology professor—finally left, more out of fatigue than anything, the bartender congratulated Ramirez on the manner in which he had held his ground. But when Ramirez woke up the next day, he was a shaken man. The situation had been distasteful, but it hadn't been the apocalypse. Why had he stayed at the bar so long, milking the episode, wallowing in it? For several days, he remained unhappy with his behavior. His life in the woods seemed tarnished. Only when he realized it was a case for Alvin Kornfeld did his mood lighten. He called the doctor, saying he was anxious to see him at long last—but there had been an unpleasant turn of events. So he had to insist the visit be on a paid professional basis. Without a struggle, Kornfeld agreed, asked him what he thought of Tokyo—and then set up an appointment.

After he hung up, Ramirez played back the bar-room episode in slow motion and quickly saw that it had been of his own making. He had felt a need for the slur and practically had to pull it out of the fellow with a pliers. His life had been going too smoothly in the woods. The professor was no innocent baby. But he had been duped into becoming Ramirez's unwitting conspirator. Once Ramirez understood this scenario, he relaxed. Obviously, there was no further need for the Kornfeld visit. But he was not about to let down his old friend either.

And so he swept into Kornfeld's office the next day, buoyant, vigorous, at the top of his form, hardly the picture of a fellow seeking improved mental health. Kornfeld, on the other hand, appeared to have gone downhill swiftly. Once robust in tennis shorts, he had aged dramatically and seemed on the edge of total collapse. His shoulders sagged, his eyes were darkly pouched. Before digging into his own situation, which for the moment seemed rosier than ever, Ramirez felt it was only fitting to ask the doctor how he was getting along—though the answer was visible on his face.

"Not so hot," said Kornfeld. Ramirez quickly had to remind himself that Kornfeld's gifts had always been conceptual—and that he had never particularly been a genius with a phrase. The poor economy had taken its toll on Kornfeld's once thriving practice. People who were only mildly upset no longer considered mental health a priority item. As a result, the haggard Kornfeld now worked nights and weekends, often at cut-rate prices; his wife, Beth Kornfeld, pitched in as a clerk in a local shoe store. No longer was Kornfeld able to take lazy August vacations collecting his beloved artifacts at the foot of extinct Mexican volcanoes. Compounding his misery was a son who had gone off the deep end, abandoning his wife and three small children, virtually depositing them as a team at Kornfeld's financial doorstep. Though this was hardly a case to make social workers weep, Ramirez felt sorry for the beleaguered doctor who had brightened his own life. The thought crossed his mind that he would send him some money— no strings attached—possibly not right away, but when he had completed work on his new copier, which was bound to put him officially in the clear.

"And how are *you* getting along, Hector?" the doctor asked after a heavy sigh.

The hour had flown by. Kornfeld had used up most of

it unburdening himself. There was no point in getting into drugs and hookers. A bump here, a bump there, he told the doctor, but for the most part, smooth sailing.

"And your work?" asked Kornfeld.

Ramirez stiffened a bit. Unmistakably, he heard a faint alarm sound in the distance. And to think, he told himself, I was almost out the door clean.

Frankly, he told the doctor, he had not been killing himself. But he *had* been working, he added quickly, on a lightweight follow-up to his triumphant 990.

"Lightweight in many ways," he said, with a chuckle. "It's designed to fit into the totebag of an executive who might, for example, be vacationing in Maui and feel a sudden urge to do a little casual copying."

The copier had some interesting features—an almost arrogant ability to reject poor copies, a mournful alarm in case of theft. But there was no question about it, he told Kornfeld. It was an amusement.

"A novelty," he said.

Kornteld did not return the chuckle. His eyes shifted slightly. How well Ramirez knew those shifts. In Kornfeld Country, they were of great significance.

"What's wrong?" he asked the doctor. "Did I say something a little off?"

"Not really," said Kornfeld as Ramirez braced himself. "It's just that...with all you know, Hector. With the reach of your mind..."

He stared out of the window. His eyes were moist.

"At one point, you were going to copy the stars."

Ramirez, suddenly in a panic, rushed to defend himself.

"I don't think you heard me correctly. I *love* my copier. I admit it's an easygoing machine. But it's just *one* copier. I expect to be making them all my life. Why does each one have to be a heavyweight?"

"Right," said Kornfeld, getting to his feet. It didn't seem

like much of an answer. Ramirez, close to fainting, asked
if the next hour happened to be free, but Kornfeld said a
divorcée was in the waiting room. Ramirez heard her pacing nervously. "She's so different from you, Hector," said
Kornfeld. "All she thinks about is money. People are so
different."

"They're also the same," said Ramirez, idiotically. It was
the last argument on God's earth he wanted to get into at
the moment. "Listen," he said, "that last thing we talked
about really upset me. I may have to see you again."

"Then you'll see me," said Kornfeld, writing down the
telephone number, which Ramirez thought he knew by
heart—although, on reflection, it turned out he didn't.

"We really do love each other," said Kornfeld, taking
him out a side door so that he wouldn't have to see the
divorcée. "We just don't know how to express it. Who
knows," he said, "perhaps it's generational."

Ramirez was weak in the knees and the fresh air he was
counting on to revive him, didn't. He thought of calling
Lucy and asking her to come get him—she would have
dropped everything and done it in a second—but decided
to try to make it on his own. He gripped the wheel of the
car so hard he almost broke it. Miraculously, he didn't drive
off the road. Kornfeld had challenged his work—the
ground he stood on. If his new Hollywood-style copier was
trivial, if indeed Kornfeld, supposedly toothless, had bur-
rowed through and found an area of moral sludge, it meant
that he had wasted a year and a half. More, actually, since
it might take him another year and a half to own up to it
and build the confidence to try still another copier. Three
years yanked out of his life, the best ones, too, the ones
just before fifty. Ramirez believed in his copier, but the
truth was, he had been tiptoeing around, waiting for a
breakthrough, waiting perhaps for the copier to break

through on its own. It was awful to admit it, but he did not have a sure grip on where he was going, the map was fuzzy and he was depending on some kind of engineering charm and insight to see him through. Who knew—perhaps the lack of economic adversity had made him smug and lazy. On the other hand, and to be a little bit more fair to himself, sudden last-minute bursts of invention had seen him through before. The copier would explain itself as it went along, announcing its intentions when it was good and ready. Until such time as it was ready to declare itself, Ramirez had to remain steady at the controls. Still, for all of this brave talk, Kornfeld had fortified doubts in his mind. By the time he got home, he was more shaken than ever. Sleep for the next few nights was out of the question. All the hugs in the world from Lucy didn't help. As a matter of fact, she even annoyed him by insisting he had gotten in a few winks. The idea of going to his shed and looking at his frail work was unthinkable. There was no point in summoning up the Kornfeld genie—he had his hands full with Kornfeld in the flesh. Yielding to the inevitable, Ramirez called the doctor to say he had to see him again, that the comments about his copier had shaken him tremendously.

Kornfeld's reaction was to chuckle softly.

"Funny," he said. "A fellow comes to a psychiatrist for help and winds up in worse shape than before."

This time it was Ramirez who didn't chuckle back.

He had been late for the last appointment. This time he was on the dot. For a horrible moment he expected Kornfeld to be hale and robust again, drawing strength from Ramirez's pain. With some relief he saw that the doctor was as haggard as he'd been the last time.

Kornfeld shook his hand and said he had told his wife that he couldn't get over what terrific shape Ramirez was in.

"And I like to think that I was just a little bit responsible."

"I'm not in such terrific shape," said Ramirez, who immediately launched an all-out defense of his new copier. Sure it was light-hearted, but he had every confidence that at any moment it would veer off into seriousness and perhaps break new ground.

"Remember my VSR-18," said Ramirez.

"Ahhhh," said Kornfeld. "Now *there* was a copier."

"And my HK-4...the big son of a bitch."

"I remember that one. *Now* you're talking copiers."

"Well, I'm *doing* that type of copier, don't you see. Except that I'm sliding into it. It has a frivolous veneer, but it might wind up with more substance than all my other copiers put together. I might even go laser with it and copy the brain itself. How'd you like a dozen neatly typed copies of some thinking you haven't even done yet? You're being taken in by the surface frivolity. But in a funny way, that may be its most important feature. All of Voltaire's heavy stuff is mouldering in the Louvre somewhere. He tossed off *Candide* as a lark, and it's the only thing of his that survives. Don't you see? The Ramirez III could wind up being the goddamned *Candide* of copiers."

"All right," said Kornfeld, awarding Ramirez his first point. "Then what was I picking up?"

"What you're picking up is that I was minimizing it at first so that you could knock it down. And then I could defend it. I do that all the time. I tried it on Lucy, but she wouldn't buy it—so I tried it on you."

"Great," said Kornfeld with a horsey grin. "Now tell me about this woman you live with. Didn't we agree she should be a professional woman, you do your thing, she does hers?"

Once again, Ramirez was stunned. First his work and now the only woman he had ever officially loved. This had started with a social visit. Where would Kornfeld draw the line? To attack Lucy, who made his heart jump every time he saw her, even if it was fifty times a day! His smile was automatic when he thought about her, even now, in the presence of Kornfeld, who had just infuriated him. Ramirez stopped strangers in the street to tell them his life began the day he met her. Sometimes he did it at parties, in front of Lucy herself. She had been on the edge of a degree in economics when he met her, then veered off and let it founder, content now to putter around in the backwoods and make his life comfortable—no small order. It's true he would have been a hair more proud of her if she had gone ahead and gotten the degree—but that was his vanity speaking.

It's possible they had settled into a routine in bed—but some routine—slow-tumbling panthers in the night. Lucy wasn't a hundred percent perfect. She walked into walls and sometimes took Ramirez with her. A massive family, dotted around the globe, made frequent visits, uncannily when Ramirez was at a critical point in his work. But they were fascinating people, all in helping professions, giving free bean sprouts to the poor in Appalachia, tending to the meek in Asia. Technically speaking, Lucy was not a Kornfeld professional, but did he know about her seriousness when she hit a tennis ball, her giggle when Ramirez told her all was lost (and didn't mean it), the almost technically perfect combination of strength and fragility in her ribs when he hugged her, the trust in her eyes (you could almost see a sign saying "trust"), the lonely war she fought to shore up his confidence in a copier he himself considered frivolous.

"That did it," said Ramirez, grabbing his coat and racing past the divorcée in the waiting room, great-eyed, genuinely sad and pretty—different from the woman he had envisioned.

"What's up," said Kornfeld, following him out to the

parking lot. "Did something I said throw you? What *does* she do?"

"I love her," said Ramirez, starting up the Saab. "That's what she does."

"What's wrong with that?" said Kornfeld. "Isn't that what it's all about? But why are you leaving this way? You'll undo fifty, maybe sixty percent of all we've achieved. Hector...Hector."

But he was too late. Ramirez tore out of the parking lot and headed for the Maine woods. Not so much to his beloved copiers, which, God have mercy on him, he realized he could live without—but to Lucy, without whom he couldn't.

—1983.

# The
# Tax Man

L OCKED IN COMBAT WITH THE government over back taxes, Ullman won some points, lost a few, but could not get the revenue service to accept his plush East Side apartment as a "working office."

"What do they think I use it for?" Ullman asked his accountant.

"They don't know," said Tisch. "They just sense it isn't for work."

"Then let them come up and see it," said Ullman. "I've got nothing to hide."

"I wouldn't do that," said the cautious Tisch. "I'd settle."

"No way," said Ullman. "I'm entitled to have whatever kind of office I like. Send 'em up."

In truth, Ullman worked a little in the apartment and played a lot. But what business was that of the government's? For all they knew, he slaved away in the place from dawn till midnight and never had any fun there. The plush decor? He needed it to put him in the mood for hard work. Howard Hughes probably had twenty such places, all over the globe, each of them a clean tax deduction. Why not one for Ullman?

On the day before the agent arrived, Ullman ran around and tried to give the place more of an office-type look. He wheeled the bar into a closet, put away his erotic statuary and scattered paperclips, rubber bands and file cards on the end tables. Here and there he set up tired piles of manuscripts.

The agent's name was Gowran, a fellow who kept his teeth gnashed together as though he were in severe abdominal pain.

"Would you like a drink?" Ullman asked him. "I don't know the protocol."

"Not just now," said Gowran, running his finger along the edge of a handsomely designed leather couch. "So this is the so-called office."

"Not so-called," said Ullman. "Just the office."

"Some place," said Gowran. "Must have cost you a bundle to furnish it."

"Not really," said Ullman. "You use tricks. Decorator short-cuts that make a little go a long way. Look, let's not fool around. This is my office. I work here. I happen to like nice surroundings. What's the government saying? That I have to work in a drab little place?"

"The government is saying take it easy," said Gowran, easing himself into a white futuristic armchair and practically disappearing in the cushions. "What about the bedroom? You work back there, too?" Ullman had hoped he wouldn't get around to that. He had devoted most of his money and effort to that room, paneling all four walls with mirrors, and the ceiling as well. He had bought the thickest rug made and put in a heavily gadgeted bed—in the great man-about-town tradition. Just his luck, the revenue agent had taken a peek at the set-up on the way into the living room. "I take naps back there," said Ullman. "Half a dozen a day. That's my style of working. Work a little, take a nap, then work some more. You want me to stop that and not take any naps, is that it?"

"Let me see your calendar," said Gowran. Ullman could not tell if he was winning or losing with this fellow, who kept his teeth gnashed together but otherwise had a neutral expression. He was prepared to go along with Gowran until the fellow stepped out of line, at which point he would ask that his case be turned over to higher-ups. Tisch had told him he could do that. But it was difficult to tell if Gowran was stepping out of line. He probably wasn't. So Ullman handed over his daily record book. He had worked on it for two weeks to make it look completely legitimate.

"You certainly take a lot of cabs," said Gowran, flipping through the diary. "No, the government isn't saying you should walk. The government is merely making an observation."

"The government is cute," said Ullman. Gowran snickered, a gray civil service exhalation of breath, and then plowed on. "Who's this guy Berger?" he asked, still studying the diary. "You've had him to lunch six times and I'm still in January. You both must be very hungry guys."

Actually, this was a break for Ullman. Most of the Berger lunches were legitimate, and in addition, he had called Berger, a public relations man, and put him on alert that the government might be in touch. And to please back him up all the way. He was in great shape on Berger, not so good on Hellwig, Danziger and Ferris, all of whom were down for fake lunches and might not come through if Gowran checked them out. "Why don't you call Phil Berger and ask him if we talked business all those times or not," said Ullman. "Here, I'll give you his number."

"That's all right," said Gowran, making a few notations in his record book and then putting it away. "Let's take a break. I know about these calendars. Everybody bullshits their way through them. You probably just got finished padding yours the second I got here. How about that drink you mentioned before?" Gowran loosened his collar, kicked out his legs and made himself comfortable. Ullman winced at the thought of this fellow with his two-bit civil service suit getting comfortable on his fine furniture, but he rushed to mix a drink all the same. If it ever got down to a pitched battle, he could say that Gowran drank on the job.

"You go to a lot of restaurants," said Gowran. "Try a place called Andy's. Terrific parmigiana and you get unlimited pasta and fruit for the same price. You get out of there, you feel like you're gonna bust."

Ullman could just about imagine what kind of place Andy's was. With its all-you-can-eat policy on pasta and fruit. He almost threw up at the thought of it, but he made believe he was jotting down the name and address for future reference.

"I don't care how many restaurants you know," he said, joining Gowran in a drink. "You can always use another one."

"Must be nice work you do," said Gowran. "Going to all those lunches and then sitting around in a place like this to do your work. With this view."

"I really do work up here," said Ullman, still defensive. "I just happen to like nice surroundings. I've worked in flophouses and now I figure I deserve this."

"Hey," said Gowran, waggling a finger. "We're taking a break, right?"

"Right," said Ullman, relaxing slightly.

"You must meet a lot of nice people," said Gowran, "a lot of good-looking chicks."

"That's right," said Ullman. "They do sort of drift into the theater if they're good-looking."

"What do you do," said Gowran, "you get these thoughts and then you sort of write them down on paper?"

"Something like that," said Ullman.

"That's nice work," said Gowran. "Hey," he said, looking at his watch and springing to his feet. "I'm supposed to meet my new girl. Can I use your phone?"

"Sure," said Ullman. "If it would make it more convenient, she can pick you up here." The drink had evidently made him feel a bit more convivial than he realized.

"That'd be terrific," said Gowran. "She'd love to see a place like this."

Gowran gave the girl the address over the phone, Ullman wondering how he could speak through those gnashed and battered teeth. He called the girl "little one," and Ullman figured this was internal revenue style. Romantic internal revenue style. He could just about imagine the girl.

Actually, she wasn't that bad. For one thing she probably should have been called "big one." She was a heavy-set girl, probably German, with languid, somewhat dazed eyes and an attractively slow-rolling style of movement. From the moment she showed up, she slowed everything in the room down. It took a few beats for Ullman to realize how attractive she was and when he did he was a little annoyed. For one thing, it had to change his view of Gowran. He had put the fellow into some kind of cramped and petty second-rate internal revenue slot. If that was his proper category, what was he doing with Ingrid? Also, it made Ullman look bad. He worked in the theater. He was supposed to be the one with Ingrids.

"The thing about this girl," said Gowran, who suddenly looked a bit dashing, "is that she'll do anything."

"Nothing bothers me," said Ingrid.

"Do something crazy," said Gowran, with a heavy-handed wink at Ullman.

Slowly, lazily, the girl stood on her hands, using Ullman's expensive bookshelves to balance herself. Her skirt poured over her head, Ullman dazzled by the erotically chunky spectacle. "It means nothing to me," said Ingrid, lightly regaining her feel after just the right amount of time and with a single movement getting her blonde hair to fall back over her shoulders. The doorbell rang and Ullman braced himself. More Ingrids? It was the dry cleaner, after Ullman's dirty suits. Ullman had them ready in a bundle and tossed it to the fellow. As the cleaner sorted it out, Gowran said, "Let's have some fun," and motioned to Ingrid. She took off her blouse, undid her bra and thrust a heavy breast against the startled dry cleaner's face. "Say," he said, "what kind of party is this?" Ingrid allowed him to enjoy it a moment and then dismissed him with a light kiss on the forehead. "She something?" said Gowran, with a chuckle.

"Whatever you like," said Ingrid, with an almost bored snap of her fingers, "I do it."

"Yet I feel sorry for the kid," said Gowran, when the puzzled dry cleaner had left. "They're going to send her back to Germany." He spoke almost as though Ingrid were not in the room.

"You said you'd get me girls," said Ingrid, removing her bra entirely now, as though it were an annoyance.

"I'm working on it," said Gowran.

"I like it with girls."

"Listen," said Gowran, "how's the grass situation up here?" The question put Ullman right on the spot. He had some, but what if he produced a few joints and Gowran slipped the cuffs on him, booking him not only on tax evasion but also on a drug rap. Maybe that's what Ingrid's presence was all about. On a simpler level—if he brought out grass it would be clear-cut evidence that the apartment was more than just an office. Still, a certain inevitability began to surround the evening. He went and got some. From the second Ingrid had walked in, he had felt a little stoned anyway. Gowran seized his joint and began to suck on it elaborately in the style of the suburban experimenter; more predictably, Ingrid declined, saying, "I don't need this. It is a waste of time. Come. What do you want to do?" She took a seat between them on the couch, cradling both Ullman's and the tax collector's head against her giant bosom and saying, "Poor babies." Ullman wasn't sure if it was the grass or a certain drugged aroma that came from the girl's flesh, but there was a jump in time, some minutes or perhaps a large part of an hour that fell out of the evening, like a skipped piece of film, and the next thing he knew the three were standing on his Swedish rug, arms around each other, none of them wearing clothes. "A little music," the tax collector whispered to Ullman. Gowran's voice, in a whisper, had none of the reedy internal revenue style to it. It was surprisingly continental. As Ullman made the adjustments on his stereo set, he became aware of a sharply attractive fragrance which he took to be Ingrid's Germanic cologne. Then, too, there was the possibility that it might be Gowran's aftershave, a subtle concoction which Ullman would never have dreamed was favored by federal tax agents. Selecting an album somewhere between hard rock and the big band sound of the forties, Ullman turned and for a panicky moment saw that the couple was gone. But then he tracked them into the bedroom and found them on his heart-shaped bed, a hundred versions of them reflected in his craftily arranged wall-and-ceiling mirrors.

Ullman slipped in beside the couple, who had begun, tentatively, without him, and soon caught their rhythm, he and the tax collector wandering across the girl's heavy-duned body, Ingrid, not bored, but somewhere beyond them, as though she were a huge piece of experiential statuary stretching herself voluptuously in the sunlight. The unspoken rules were that Ullman and the tax man were to make love to her, but that both were to occupy separate zones and never to make contact with one another. Until one moment, deep in the night, when Ullman heard the revenue man whisper "over this way" and it seemed natural to alter the rules somewhat and finally, to abandon them altogether. And then, in an even deeper chamber of the night, the girl was gone and Ullman could recall no effort on either his or Gowran's part to keep her there.

In the morning, Ullman awoke with an awareness that he had not slept very long. At the same time, he felt none of the staleness that generally went with lack of sleep. A moment later, Gowran, fully dressed except for the thin civil service necktie, stood above him with an open can of condensed milk, wanting to know if it was fresh enough to use with his coffee. "I think it's okay," said Ullman. He

brushed his teeth then, put in his contact lenses and showered, deliberately keeping his thoughts vague in the stream
of hot water and preferring not to confront just yet the
central new fact of his existence: that no matter how he
sliced it, he had spent half the night in a tax collector's
arms. After changing the sheets and making the bed, he
dressed, making sure that everything he wore was spot-
lessly new and clean—and then he appeared in the breakfast alcove.

"Get some sleep?" asked Gowran, sipping his coffee and
riffling through Ullman's daily record book, making a note
or two.

"Not bad," said Ullman. "What happened to your girl
friend?"

"Nice kid, huh?" said Gowran. "She had an appointment.
You want to start now or get some breakfast first? I've got
some questions about April 1968. Your figures don't add
up."

"All right, hold it right there," said Ullman, pouring
some juice and then slamming down the container. "I don't
think you quite realize what's happened. You know, I just
don't do this. This is a very big thing to me. I've never
done this in my life. I won't kid you, I've had the thought
a few times and maybe I even knew that some day I'd get
around to it and give it a try. But I've never actually done
it before. Never even come near it. This is a very strong
new thing for me. I haven't even begun to assess the effect
of it yet. I may not even be able to function normally when
it hits me. My whole personality could be out the window.
For Christ's sakes, I haven't done anything like this since
Roger Lacey in Bunk Nine at Camp Deerfleet and that
was nothing compared to last night. That was just a harm-
less little cupcake. For all I know this may turn out to be
the single most shattering thing I've ever done in my thir-

ties. I may get a goddamned nervous breakdown over last night and you want to casually jump in and review calendar notes for April '68."

"That's right," said Gowran, munching on a toasted English muffin and turning the pages of Ullman's diary until he came to the page he wanted. "Now who's this fellow Benziger and what do you fellows find to talk about three times a week at expensive French restaurants?"

"Bitch," said Ullman and was shocked by the unmistakably female hiss that accompanied the outburst.

—1977.

# Detroit
# Abe

**A**LONE, FRIGHTENED, POUNDED ON THE head by alimony, the IRS circling closer, Abrahamowitz almost considered going back to the synagogue. Once in a while he would walk by one, take a peek inside, and keep going. They weren't going to get him just yet. The ground was crumbling beneath his feet. If the roof ever collapsed, he would barge in, perhaps during the High Holidays, and say, "How about taking me back?" To the best of his knowledge they would have to, unless it was an expensive one that could keep him out with prohibitive dues. Once it had been his dream to end his days as an aging boulevardier at the Gritti Hotel in Venice, staring at the Canal.

"Who is he?" a tourist would ask the maître d'.

"The American," would be the reply. "They say he was once a literary fellow, an intimate of both Roths, Henry and Philip. Now he just orders a Negroni and sits and stares at the Canal. I think he is waiting for the contessa, but she will not come."

But at the rate he was going, Abrahamowitz was not going to make it to Venice. Where would he get the fare? How could he calm down enough to make the trip over? The chances were strong that it would be the synagogue after all, his ace in the hole.

He taught irony to a group of students in a heavily ethnic division of a city university. And he taught a lot of it, too, three separate courses: Classical Irony, Eighteenth-Century Irony, and Contemporary Irony. Why did they need so much irony? And why Abrahamowitz to teach it, when his real strength was in War Fiction, a course he could not get approved by the department because of the Vietnam experience? He was sturdy in contemporary irony,

held his own in the eighteenth century, and, by his own
admission, disgraced himself in the classics. His classes were
packed with students, the overflow spilling out into the
halls. Weeks into the semester, a half dozen more would
transfer from Spenser seminars. He couldn't figure out
why everyone wanted to get into irony. They were poor
kids; shouldn't they be learning how to run small busi-
nesses—or at least mastering the fundamentals of hospital
supply? Exactly where were they going with *Candide* and
*A Tale of a Tub?* How were they going to throw *A Vindication
of Isaac Bickerstaff, Esq.* into practical application?

Abrahamowitz was afraid of his students. Even though
great armies of them poured into his classes, once installed,
they would sit and stare blankly at him. What were they
thinking? That he was an idiot? He had no way of knowing.
He would ask a question—"Is literary irony a positive or
negative force?"—then sit back, arms folded, determined
to sweat them out. But after a few beats he would become
terrified and push on with the answer, which was that he
wasn't sure—it could be either.

Outside, an elevated train—one of the few remaining
in the city—roared by every five minutes, invariably
drowning out his best material. Also, the seats in the classroom were arranged in maddeningly straight, geometrically precise lines and riveted to the floor. Abrahamowitz
yearned to yank them free and scatter them about—but
the dean said that an expensive departmental study had
advocated neat rows (as a pathway to neat thinking) and
that he wasn't allowed to.

He taught four days a week and spent the other three
getting ready for the four. He lived alone in a one-room
apartment, his only luxury a huge Sony television set that
he never turned on. Often he sat and stared at the blank
screen, which was somewhat relaxing. He used this as an
example of irony to one of his classes, the staring at a blank

set. Their reaction was to stare back blankly at him. Maybe it wasn't ironic enough for them. He lived alone because women had always deserted him at critical junctures in his life. His wife told him she wanted a divorce as he was being wheeled in for a hemorrhoid operation. A longtime girl friend walked out just as he was leaving to deliver the most important lecture of his life, at Notre Dame, replacing a Polish novelist who had gone through the windshield of an Alfa Romeo. His delivery was shaky, and when he got back, the lecture bureau struck his name from the catalog. (He had to admit there had been one good moment, when an old poet cried out to him as he boarded the train: "You've got something fine. Hold on to it. I never could.") So he had little to do with women. His sex came to him through magazines, lately ones in which women were tied to brooms.

Each night, drained from teaching, Abrahamowitz would take a little nap and then eat dinner alone at a restaurant, usually one of the city's colorful ethnic ones—since, amazingly, in spite of leading what he saw as a harsh, nervous life, he was blessed with an iron stomach. So, in the event he went wrong on a Filipino delicacy, he didn't suffer as much as the next man. One particular night he selected a new and somewhat high-priced establishment that featured the foods of north India. Plushly decorated, boasting authentic clay ovens, and highly recommended by a leading restaurant guide, the place had quickly caught fire. Since the dining room on this particular occasion was overflowing with customers, Abrahamowitz, a single, was asked by the management if he would mind having his dinner in the lounge.

"It's all right with me," he said, and was led to a small table in the corner. Seated in a booth next to him was a pleasant-looking young black man with a jeweled pendant around his neck and a smashingly lovely, though somewhat vacant-looking, young white girl at his side. She had long, black hair, and when she got up to go to the ladies' room, Abrahamowitz noticed that she was just a fraction too plump around the bottom—in other words, his favorite physical type if he had been interested in women, which he wasn't. Possibly he had been more aware of the couple than he realized; otherwise he would never have noticed the long pause that followed when the waiter asked them what they would like for dinner. Not thinking much of this, and feeling a little buzz from his second J & B Scotch sour on the rocks, Abrahamowitz abandoned his normal reticence to lean over and say, "I hear the tandoori chicken is marvelous." The black man glanced neutrally in his direction but did not respond. Yet when Abrahamowitz turned away he heard the fellow say, "I believe we'll both have the tandoori chicken." Roughly an hour later, the black man sent his girl friend off with a light tap on that terrific behind; then, with an appealing shyness, he asked Abrahamowitz to join him for a drink.

"Delighted," said Abrahamowitz.

"I'm Smooth," said the fellow, extending a gentle hand.

"Irwin Abrahamowitz. How do you do?"

Both men, strangely enough, loved the same drink, sombreros—Kahlúa with a little white "hat" of sweet cream on top—and this is what they ordered.

"First off," said Smooth, "I want to thank you for saving my ass."

"For what?" said Abrahamowitz. "Telling you about the chicken? That's ridiculous."

But it wasn't so ridiculous to Smooth, who explained that he was involved in pimping, that his companion was the number-one girl in his stable, and that the moment after the waiter had asked for his order had been one of the most terrifying ones of his life.

"How come?" asked Abrahamowitz.

"My cool was in danger. If I had said something dumb, Diane would have picked up on it. Next morning she'd be over working with my archrival, French Fries."

By way of further explanation, Smooth told Abrahamowitz that "cool" was the most important element in his profession. This was particularly true in his case, since he never smacked his girls around or razor-marked them in the style of French Fries, his competitor. On the contrary, he treated them with kindness and had even set up a retirement plan in which over-the-hill ones were given boutiques. Hence the nickname Smooth.

"So I'm very grateful to you," said Abrahamowitz's new friend.

"Glad I was able to help."

"What profession are you in, may I ask?"

Abrahamowitz said that he was the visiting irony professor at Monrose College, adding, reflexively, that he was underpaid and that in spite of it they were working him like a dog.

"A way to spot irony," he explained to Smooth, who hadn't asked, "is when you can't quite make out the intentions of the author and when the hero ends up in puzzled defeat." Smooth considered this momentarily, then said that he himself was trying to shift over to the recording business as a hedge against his middle years and the possibility of the pimping business going sour.

"Would you care to step out to my car and listen to one of my tunes?"

Abrahamowitz, slightly edgy, with an eight-in-the-morning class coming up the next day, said all right but that he couldn't stay long. Smooth got up quickly and led the way, Abrahamowitz dropping a few dollars on the table to pay for the sombreros. The mild-mannered young man then escorted Abrahamowitz to an old Dodge, explaining that his real car, a forty-five-thousand-dollar reconverted Bentley pimpmobile, was in the shop for repairs. In the front seat of the Dodge the two listened to a tape of "Checkin' My Birds," which had been written and produced by Smooth. The number was catchy and melodious. Abrahamowitz admired particularly the falsetto of the lead singer, who turned out to be Smooth himself. Smooth explained that for a brief period he had been one of the Milk Duds, a group doing club dates out of South Philly.

"Do you have any connections in the recording business?"

It seemed a strange question to be asking Abrahamowitz, an irony man whose life was bounded on the one side by Juvenal, on the other by *The Cankered Muse*. Abrahamowitz shared a desk in the faculty lounge with Ostrow, a Dryden man and a cellist who, as a favor to the music section, occasionally covered Harmonics I; but he was hardly the man Smooth was after. Besides, they fought bitterly over the desk, Ostrow continually trying to get extra drawer space.

"Frankly, nobody comes to mind," said Abrahamowitz.

"That's perfectly all right," said Smooth, who certainly did have a sweet disposition. "May I give you a lift home?"

"That would be lovely."

As they drove along Abrahamowitz found himself humming the infectiously catchy "Checkin' My Birds." Fleetingly, he wondered why—if Smooth was so grateful to him—he didn't offer to send over the girl with the slightly heavy behind, even for half an hour, which was the absolute limit on time he could spare from his classroom preparation. As they reached the front door of Abrahamowitz's West Side apartment they shook hands, Smooth once again thanking him for bailing him out of a tight spot. Abrahamowitz got out of the car.

"Incidentally," said Smooth, leaning out of the window,

"did you notice how I didn't offer to send over the girl, even though you did me a big turn?"

"Yes, frankly, I noticed that."

"Another thing. I have a whole pile of money in here with me. Did you wonder why I let you spring for the drinks?"

"That crossed my mind, too."

"Well, let me ask you a question," said Smooth, his brows furrowed in thought.

"Go right ahead."

"Is that what you mean by irony?"

And that was the last he had seen or heard of Smooth, even though he occasionally found himself humming the damnably catchy "Checkin' My Birds." One morning several weeks later, Abrahamowitz was rushing through a second cup of coffee at the Delicatessen Elegante when his eye fell upon a *Times* news story that told of the roundup and indictment of seven of the city's leading pimps. There were photographs of each of these fellows, and the one that registered immediately was that of Arthur Taylor, age twenty-seven, who resided at Henry's Motor Lodge in midtown Manhattan. There was no doubt that this was the person Abrahamowitz knew as Smooth, his friend from the Indian restaurant. According to the *Times* crime blotter, the mild-mannered fellow, along with the others, was under criminal indictment on the grounds of income tax evasion. Staring him in the face: A sentence of three to seven years in a federal penitentiary. Further along, the story said that Arthur Taylor had first come under suspicion as a result of a radio interview in which he let slip that he earned a quarter of a million dollars a year and hardly lifted a finger to get it, rising each day at noon. What an idiotic thing to admit to on the public airwaves! Some downtrodden, overworked IRS sleuth earning four-

teen thousand nine hundred ninety-nine dollars per an-
num (Abrahamowitz's salary to the penny, incidentally)
must have been tuned in and gotten infuriated. The last
line of the story indicated that one of Arthur Taylor's girls
was ready to testify that she handed over fifteen thousand
dollars in cash to the pimp, the IRS insisting there wasn't
a penny of tax paid on this amount.

It was late, and Abrahamowitz would have to race to the
subway to make it out to Monrose College on time. He had
no irony to teach on this particular day, but he was expected to show up at a meeting to discuss faculty dental
benefits. As he took a last sip of coffee Abrahamowitz
wondered if Smooth would be able to sweet-talk his way
past the homosexuality that was so rampant in the prison
system, or if he would be turned briskly into a fag. Noting
with irritation that juice had gone up a dime, he paid his
check to Seitz, the owner, a ferocious reader of bestsellers
who knew Abrahamowitz was in literature. "What'd you
think of *Princess Daisy?*" asked Seitz, ringing up the $2.85
for juice, eggs, and coffee. What was Abrahamowitz supposed to do—give him a quick critique with forty people
listening in, not to mention the countermen? "I didn't read
it," Abrahamowitz lied. "Wait till you do," said Seitz. "You'll
piss." Abrahamowitz ducked out, not allowing Seitz to get
started on his daughter, who was an artist in Los Angeles
and designed drapes. "If you're ever in L.A.," Seitz would
say, "I want you to see those drapes." That's just what
Abrahamowitz wanted to do—look at Gloria Seitz's drapes
in L.A.

On the subway out to Monrose, guarding his briefcase
so that no one could snatch it, Abrahamowitz decided that
the girl who had ratted on Smooth was probably the one
with the lazy, magnificent behind. After all the nice things
Smooth had done for her, coldly and perversely she had

gone to the tax boys and turned him in. Exactly Abrahamowitz's experience with the fair sex.

Later in the day, Abrahamowitz sat in his tiny English department office, filling out a long dental-care form. Actually, it wasn't that great a plan. The first twenty fillings were on the subscriber; after that the insurance company took over. Only if you came into the plan with a smashed mouth or teeth decayed by long periods of malnutrition did it make any sense. Still, it was on the house, so he filled out the form anyway. In the back of his mind he was thinking about the three students who had spent a month in one of his irony courses under the impression that they were in Intermediate Logic. Whose fault was it? Were they really paying attention? Not only had they petitioned out of the class, but they had complained to Dean Kiltar that their sense of logic had been thrown off. If that was the case, why didn't they stay in irony? Who asked them to leave? These were his thoughts as the phone rang and he received, not with total surprise, a call from his troubled acquaintance.

"Abrim..."

"Yes?"

"This is Smooth."

"Nice to hear from you," said Abrahamowitz. "How are things going?" he asked, knowing full well they were going lousy.

"Just fine. I wonder if you could spare me a few moments of your time."

"Of course," said Abrahamowitz. "How about drinks and dinner at the Punjab again. I haven't been there in a long time and I could use a little Indian food."

"Actually, I'm a little pressed for time. I'm in your neighborhood and I wonder if I could drop by in the next hour."

Abrahamowitz was more or less free, but he was not

thrilled by the prospect of the indicted pimp showing up
in the English department. So he named a restaurant six
blocks away. "The food isn't so hot in this neighborhood,"
he said, "but this particular place is first rate, because it's
right near the courthouse, and you know lawyers. They
won't stand for anything but the best."

"Half an hour," said Smooth.

As he walked past row upon row of cut-rate furniture
stores, religious-medallion stores, and pizza parlors Abrahamowitz felt a drumming of both excitement and apprehension at the prospect of meeting Smooth. He had never
spent time with an indicted fellow. What did Smooth want
from him? Money? That was ridiculous, since by his own
admission the industrious young flesh peddler had tons of
it. Legal counsel? Abrahamowitz, in his divorce, had been
represented by a firm that was so exalted and dignified
that he himself was afraid to call them up or visit them.
Billings, Cohen and LeTournier represented corporations,
retired diplomats, entire western states that were in bound-
ary disputes with adjoining territories. How would it look
to show up at their offices with Smooth, even though he
wasn't exactly ashamed of him? Abrahamowitz felt the reason he was always in such hot water in the alimony department was that he was too embarrassed to take up any
of the law firm's time. What if he asked them a lowly
question about alimony reduction, threw off their rhythm
and as a result a northern county of Oklahoma lost its
natural gas rights to a greedy neighbor. So he couldn't
help the troubled pimp in this department. Maybe Smooth
simply wanted the comfort of being with an older-brother
type and a friend, which, of course, was preposterous. With
his street-wise intelligence, surely he had grasped the fact
that Abrahamowitz was a loner, temporarily—perhaps
permanently—sealed off from the world, unable to give

help or solace to any other human being except perhaps a tiny little bit to his ex-family.

At the JuryBox Restaurant, Smooth wasted little time in getting to the point. Before the waiter arrived to take their lunch order, the soft-spoken pimp said that he was going to be taking a little vacation in the near future.

"I'll be going away for from three to seven..."

"So I've heard," said Abrahamowitz.

"What do you mean?" said Smooth, with a sharpness Abrahamowitz hadn't seen before. Apparently he was touchy about his legal situation. Abrahamowitz saw that he would have to tread softly. He also decided Smooth would be able to take care of himself in prison.

"I hadn't exactly *heard*," said Abrahamowitz. "I just figured you fellows get a lot of leisure time."

Smooth cocked his head quizzically, making a judgment. After a few beats he relaxed and offered his proposal.

"How'd you like to take over the operation for a while? During the period I'm in absentia?"

"I don't follow you," said Abrahamowitz, who was actually following him very closely. "What do you mean?"

"You know, run the game. Take care of the birds, check the traps, do the collecting. Half goes to you and you hold my half till I return from resting up."

"I don't know anything about such things," said Abrahamowitz, sneaking a hand over to his chest to check his heartbeat. "I've got my teaching—"

"There's not much to it," said Smooth. "I can go into the details later. I just wanted to get a sense of your general reaction."

"I hardly know what to say," said Abrahamowitz, who, as Smooth must have noted, did not give him a flat-out no. "How would it be for a college professor to be a pimp? Incidentally, I hope you don't mind my use of the word."

"That's perfectly all right," said Smooth. "You see, that's

why I figured you'd be effective. Nobody would be quick
to put you together with the game."

"The last thing I am is smooth," said Abrahamowitz, a
bit weakly.

"You're smoother than you think, Abrim." With that,
Smooth picked up a shoe box he had brought along and
gestured discreetly toward the men's room.

"Come along inside there with me," said Smooth. "I'd
like to show you something."

"What have you got, a hot watch?" said Abrahamowitz,
a nervously lame joke that Smooth beat back with a cool
glance. The pimp then led the way to the rest room; Abrahamowitz followed, eyes on the mysterious shoe box,
recalling for an instant Abrahamowitz & Sons, the
medium-huge empire of his forebears that had ruled the
Lower East Side hosiery game until the four shiftless and
lazy Abrahamowitz brothers (his uncles and his own dad)
let it go to seed. Inside, Smooth peered around to make
sure there were no eavesdropping lawyers in the stalls.
Satisfied they were alone, he lifted the lid of the box and
showed Abrahamowitz the contents: bills, in individual
stacks, tied together with string. They were weathered and
tragic-looking bills, indeed, but Abrahamowitz spotted
batches of fifties, not to mention a thick border of hundreds
along the sides.

"Now, this here is the type of money the operation gets
involved with," said Smooth. He might have been a salesman showing Abrahamowitz slacks. "What you're looking
at, for example, is fifty thousand dollars, which is the take
for the bimonthly period." Outside of the movies, it was
the most cash Abrahamowitz had ever seen. His own yearly
full-time-professor's salary? It could have filled a match-
box. He had to restrain an impulse to reach in, take a
fistful and worry about the consequences later. A lawyer
came in to use the urinal and Smooth quickly snapped the

box shut. "I've secreted the widow in a remote section of Long Island," Smooth said, adopting a barrister's tone, "while the battle over trustees ensues." Smooth certainly did think with lightning speed. Abrahamowitz tried desperately to think of something legalistic to say in reply. "Torts," he hollered out finally, causing the urinating attorney to wheel around.

"So what do you think, Abrim," said Smooth when they had returned to their table. He rocked his chair back and snapped his fingers to get the waiter's attention. "You in or you out?"

"I guess I'd better say out," said Abrahamowitz.

"I didn't ask what you'd *better* say," said Smooth, with a slight trace of contempt. "I asked what *do* you say."

"I can't handle it," said Abrahamowitz.

"Tell you what," said Smooth. "Take a couple of days to think it over. I'll be occupied with making preparations for my trip anyway. Then you let me know." He did some scribbling on a matchbook, which he then handed to Abrahamowitz. "Now here's three numbers. You can reach me at one of them. Deal?"

"Deal," said Abrahamowitz, who always leapt at a chance to put off a decision.

The waiter appeared and handed them menus.

"Don't even bother to read it," said Abrahamowitz. "I know what's good. Take the stuffed derma."

Smooth raised his head slowly and fixed Abrahamowitz with a look so terrifying that he no longer feared for the pimp but for the other prisoners. Then, not taking his eyes off Abrahamowitz for an instant, he addressed the waiter.

"I'll have the cheese blintzes, a double order of kasha varnishkes, and a diet celery tonic."

For the next several days, Abrahamowitz wrestled with the sweet-talking Smooth's proposition. Should he give him a flat-out no, or try his hand at the pimping game? On the one hand, it was preposterous—a man of letters overseeing a troupe of hookers. He would be out of business in a week. (Abrahamowitz had noted, incidentally, that Smooth's rival, the vicious French Fries, so quick to use a razor, had eluded the police roundup.) On the other hand, there was the shoe box full of money, which represented a mere taste of Smooth's annual gross receipts. Even a handful would solve so many of his problems—bring him up to date on alimony and enable him to move out of his stuffy one-room rear apartment and perhaps put a deposit down on a terrific three-roomer he had looked at wistfully, one with a charming glassed-in French dining area in a reconverted town house. And there would be money left over for that battered, windswept house he was almost positive he wanted on a deserted section of the Maine coastline.

Still, Smooth's proposition, to put it mildly, represented a minefield of dangers. If word ever leaked out, he would be finished in higher education. But to look at it another way: Where exactly was he going in higher education? For sixteen years he had kicked around on grubby little fellowships and temporary appointments. Like an idiot, he had never signed up for a pension plan—the forms were too complicated. He had put in three years at Monrose, but there wasn't a chance in hell that Dean Kiltar would allow him to achieve tenure. Anyone who had been present when Kiltar observed his Classical Irony session and listened to Abrahamowitz make a hash of Juvenal's Third Satire could have told you this.

Then there was the moral and ethical question, of which he had barely scratched the surface. Again he thought of the bills in Smooth's shoe box. Did he want to achieve financial security through money that had lonely dreams and come on it? He tried to view this in another light: the girls had presumably given pleasure, gotten some cash for themselves. If they were Smooth's girls, it was a safe guess that they had not hit their customers on the head. In the great universal scheme, who had actually suffered?

Setting aside questions of morality for the moment, there was the hard issue of criminal behavior. If a girl had ratted on the street-wise Smooth, why wouldn't another spill the beans on the outrageously naive Abrahamowitz? He would wind up in a cell right next to Smooth. Abrahamowitz was of two minds about prison—as he was about everything else. On the one hand, he might finally get some peace and quiet. But what if he got a sudden urge for a cheeseburger one night and found the guards unsympathetic? He knew himself. He would smash his head against the bars. Add to this the fact that if Smooth was even a marginal candidate for homosexuality, Abrahamowitz was a dead duck. They'd have him turned into a gay the second he set foot inside prison walls. He had devoted a great deal of thought to this subject and come to the conclusion that it was not his cup of tea. (Maybe years later, in Naples, with an urchin.)

On the subject of hookers in general, Abrahamowitz, were the truth to be told, was not so naive as his professorial demeanor might have indicated. He'd had quite a little romance with them over the years, starting with a pair of teenage sisters he had encountered while on a fellowship at the University of Puerto Rico. "Fucky, fucky," the older one whispered in his left ear; "Sucky, sucky," her sister said in his other ear; and for fifty dollars he was off to the races. For ten years, every once in a while he would slip off and find a hooker, and this was not because his marriage was shaky. He liked the very coldness of the transaction. As a youngster, growing up in Queens, he often felt he would lay down his life for a single glimpse of the outer aureole of one of Kathryn Grayson's filmdom breasts.

For him it remained miraculous that he could simply plunk down some money to buy a strange woman's body, getting aureoles to his heart's content—imagining, if he preferred, that they were those of the imperious Grayson herself. Some said what good was it—you couldn't buy the girl's soul. That was the whole point. What did he need her soul for? Where was he going with it? In truth, Abrahamowitz would still be going to hookers if it hadn't been for a chance remark he had overheard in a cafeteria: "Hookers don't work hard enough for their money." The truth was: Some did and some didn't. But that was a side issue. He liked the sound of the remark and stopped going to them. That's the way he was—he would change the course of his life on the basis of a stray bit of wisdom, one he had reached out and caught as if it were a fly ball. Also, giving up hookers gave him a chance to renounce another pleasure—for Abrahamowitz, a pleasure in itself.

Though he kept focusing on the shoe box loaded with soiled but tax-free fifties and hundreds, it was not so much the money that kept him toying with Smooth's proposition. In one corridor of himself, he enjoyed being hard-pressed and financially put upon. For all his complaining, he had heat and shelter and ate in ethnic restaurants that weren't exactly dirt cheap. At some point later in his life he might want to take a round-the-world cruise, but he was in no hurry. His clothes, for some mysterious reason, never wore out; vainly he waited for sweaters that were seventeen years old to get a little frayed around the sleeves. The fact that he was always behind in alimony to his wife, who had fled with his daughters to sunny California, gave him shivers of martyrdom.

It was not, finally, the dollars that made him vulnerable to Smooth's farfetched proposition. Taking a cold look at his life, Abrahamowitz could see clearly that his options were running out. He was forty-eight. One by one his dreams had been picked off at the plate. He still felt there was poetry in him, but it was too late to pry it out. At thirty-eight, yes. At forty-eight, no. When his wife had fled to the West Coast during his hemorrhoid operation, he dreamed, upon recovery, of a shy, scholary, flaxen-haired girl who would take her place, occupying a quietly supportive corner of his life. He was still waiting—but he no longer held his breath.

Apart from certain hotly spiced ethnic foods, life no longer had any taste to it. He lacked the ambition to turn on the TV set. One by one his friends drifted away when he didn't return their calls, not that he'd had a crowd of them to begin with.

He had loved his daughters but he noticed that when the summers came he didn't rush to the West Coast to see them, even though he could have gotten a special professor's ticket discount. He was an "old" forty-eight. Like an idiot, he asked strangers how old he looked, and most guessed fifty-five. As a desperate measure he had shaved off his beard, and came out looking older. What was left for him? Walks in the park? Marriage to a middle-aged psychiatrist with a stock portfolio and a thick waistline? It was true that he enjoyed some measure of success as a teacher and that students, mysteriously, flocked from far and wide to attend his irony classes. But how could he account for their collectively hollow look while he struggled to be charming and ironic? And if they loved irony so much, why was there a groan when he sneaked an extra book into the syllabus, an Evelyn Waugh they might love?

Still and all, after weighing the pluses and minuses of Smooth's offer, he came to the only possible conclusion for a civilized man—no soap. The idea of becoming a middle-aged pimp while continuing to teach a full schedule at Monrose College was preposterous. And this is exactly what he intended to convey to the well-intentioned Smooth, when a little birdie whispered into his ear: "Abrahamowitz. Don't be a fool. You're leading a stuffy and selfish life. Let a little air in. All you are doing is tap-dancing, waiting around to die. Time is running out. Take a shot."

It was late at night, and he had stopped at a corner pay telephone, one of the few in the neighborhood that had not been ripped out by vandals. He tried one number, then a second and finally reached Smooth at the third. Henry's Motor Lodge, room 1214. "Who's this speaking?" asked Smooth.

Abrahamowitz said nothing.

"Who is this?"

More silence while he flailed about for terminology.

And then, a beat later, with a knot at the end of his voice, Abrahamowitz spoke.

"Smooth?"

"Yes, yes, who *is* it?"

Abrahamowitz let out a long, deep sigh, hesitated one last time, then dove in.

"This is Detroit Abe."

—1973.

# King
# of the
# Bloodies

ONE BY ONE, SHORTNER'S CHILDHOOD friends drifted away. The closest to him, Gribetz, fleeing a bad marriage, disappeared in the Midwest, taking work as a lab technician. Saddler, handsome, confident, turned up, predictably, as a heart specialist in the Philadelphia area. Hammer, of all people, became a West Coast tycoon, specializing in elevator equipment. And he had been the worst athlete on the block, the last to be chosen in all games. God only knew what became of McKeown and Billets. Then there was Marse, not that close a friend, but a definite presence in Shortner's childhood. He remembered Marse gliding by the drugstore, a short, almost geometrically squared-off fellow carrying a briefcase, tossing a brusque nod toward the boys on the corner, then marching off, presumably to get a jump on life. He had seemed middle-aged as a child. Some claimed he was selling insurance and that there were endowment policies in the briefcase. Shortner kept tabs on Marse, as if there were any way to avoid it. A brief but brilliant career in law, another as a political columnist—and then Marse had been snapped up as the drama critic for a powerful daily newspaper, one that was able to pronounce life or death sentences on incoming Broadway plays. This was Marse's job when Shortner ran into him at a junior high school reunion. The speakers were four district attorneys, each having his say about the rise of youth gangs in the area. Shortner was amazed the school had produced so many district attorneys. And he wondered why a more balanced program of speakers couldn't have been served up. Marse evidently felt the same way; he eased his chair closer to Shortner's so they could have a whispered conversation. Marse's wife eased closer, too. Attractive in a swarthy way, she seemed troubled, as though Marse, in his brusque and confident march through life, had rarely slowed down to minister to her feminine needs. It was the same old Marse, stocky, squared-off, middle-aged, except that now he *was* middle-aged. For a moment, Shortner thought he might be wearing one of his old boyhood blue suits. "I see we're being very district attorney tonight," said Marse. Though the remark might have been considered waspish, Marse's tone itself was gentle. This came as a surprise to Shortner, who expected that he would be lordly and imperious. Three dazzling careers had evidently given him the confidence to be easygoing. Shortner asked Marse how he was, as if he didn't know. Marse said tip-top and asked the same question of Shortner, who was getting along, but not setting the world on fire either as an editor of technical manuals. "Then you've given up writing?" said Marse, half turning to his wife, as if he had unearthed some extraordinary news. What writing, Shortner wondered. Could he possibly have meant the junior high school column he had once written, called *Shorties from Shortner,* a series of one-line shafts about life in America? Rereading them years later, Shortner saw clearly that most had missed the mark. "I'm not doing any," said Shortner.

"Then why don't you come write a play?" asked Marse. Come where, Shortner was about to ask, but held back. Why be a wise ass when Marse, with far sturdier credentials, was being straightforward?

"I don't have an idea," said Shortner, as the second D.A. hopped up to the podium, "and I don't know how to write one." Actually, only the second part was true. He did have an idea, or at least a notion. Bringing it off was another story.

"That doesn't seem to be stopping most people these days."

Once wishy-washy, Shortner, in his forties now, had

learned a new trick: Bluntness. As a younger man, his fear had been that if he said something in a clear and direct way, people on the receiving end would throw things at him. Only once in a while had this happened. So he had eased into a new style, at first prefacing his candid remarks with the phrase, "To be perfectly blunt," then not even bothering with the prefaces. He would simply plunge in, as he did, on this occasion, with Marse.

"Are you saying," he asked Marse, "that if I wrote a play, the fix would be in?"

"To be blunt about it," said Marse, amazingly not shielding the remark from his wife, who was probably too deep in her own swarthy worries to care, "yes."

"I might take a shot at it," said Shortner.

"Do," said Marse, abruptly turning his attention to the speaker's platform, his first imperious gesture of the evening.

In the weeks to come, Shortner foamed over with confusion and excitement. Luckily, he could do his technical manuals with one hand tied behind his back. Once he had apologized to his boss for being in a temporary depression. "Even at fifty percent," said the head man, "you're better than most of my guys at a hundred." Somehow, none of Shortner's anxieties had to do with the possibility that Marse might be toying around with him. The man was too big for that sort of nonsense. What concerned him was his own ability to produce a workable dramatic piece. It was one thing to have an idea for a play—very romantic—quite another to actually plunge in and get it written. And how about that idea. Blood. That is, the subculture of the small-time banks and the down-and-outers who sold their blood for survival. The piece would pivot around one tough, skinny fellow from the West Coast named Sailor who was known to the flophouse crowd as "King of the Bloodies," a man who had come up with more pints to sell than anyone in the country. Lean, grizzled, wiry, no more than a hundred and twenty pounds, he seemed bloodless, yet, when something was at stake, there was always one pint to be squeezed out of his veins. The play would have to do with Sailor showing up in the East, learning that an old-timer friend of his named Cactus was sick and in deep trouble. Sailor, not in very good shape himself, would try to bail out his old buddy by coming up with a few pints and selling them.

Maybe he would lose his life in trying to squeeze out that last drop, maybe not. There were several possible endings. But there didn't seem to be any beginning. The idea was close to satire, Shortner realized that. Except that he believed in his tough and knotty little hero. The idea was to get him on paper. After a week of writing through sleepless nights, Shortner, with great relief, gave up. And having officially given up, he was able to begin. He thought it would take a year to write a play, a minimum of six months. It took him three days and nights which meant, of course, that it was lousy. Or did it? Whom could he show it to? His boss, an overseer of technical manuals in the electrical field? For one thing, it might jeopardize his job, all that work on the side. His wife? She would study his eyes and figure out what he wanted to hear. Wonderful? You got it. How about Marse? As long as the arrangement was so blunt, why not lay it right on the man who had encouraged him in the first place? Getting blunter and blunter by the moment, he called Marse and said, "I've written one. Will you read it?"

"Cart it over here," said Marse. They met at a French restaurant, Marse's choice, and surprisingly second-rate at that. A green, almost laminated sauce was poured on all entrées. But Shortner wasn't there to eat. Besides, Marse had picked the restaurant because it was out of the way, and they could be free of the inquisitive stares of people in the theater business. Yet, surprisingly, they weren't that free; Shortner recognized a few actors and producers scattered about, all putting up with the green sauce and, who knows, maybe even loving it. Right out there in the open, Marse whipped through the script, chuckling here and there while Shortner, nibbling on a salad, tried to guess which lines were tickling him. Half an hour later, Marse stacked up the pages evenly and said, "Frankly, I'd expected something a bit more Shavian (*Shorties from Shortner?*) but I liked it. It's fresh and I think it'll play."

"What do you mean you *think?*" said Shortner.

"I know it will play."

"What do I do now?"

"Follow me," said Marse, leading Shortner over to a great ruin of a man who had been sitting on the edge of the restaurant, pretending not to notice anyone, but probably clocking every second of the action. This was Koner, a producer with a blemished but long record in theater.

"Say hello to Shortner," said Marse, "an old school chum. He's written a brilliant play, the one in my hand here, and I think you should produce it."

Shortner's eyes almost fell out of his head over the bluntness of it all. And he thought *he* was blunt. So this is how things were done in the theater. Right out in the open. What about Albee and Williams? Had their towering successes been hooked into deals made openly in restaurants? Shortner wasn't asking any questions. And produce the play Koner did. Shortner was never sure if he liked it. Or if he had read it. It had come gift-wrapped with a note from the most powerful drama critic in the world, the very man who would be sitting fourth row on the aisle, opening night, ready to say thumbs up or thumbs down. And he had pretty much spelled out the way he intended to go. That was enough for Koner. Within a week a director had been hired and Shortner was busy rewriting, little feathery rewrites that were fun and only one bold one, putting the second act first and the first second. Marse popped into the producer's office one day, demanding to see the rewrites. He insisted that the acts be reversed again. Wasn't he petrified that some keen-eyed young reporter might spot him and blow the whistle? Evidently not. Perhaps he was counting on the very boldness of his actions to throw people off. It was as if the secretary of state were brazenly picking up hookers in broad daylight.

Shortner plunged ahead with his light rewrites. New to playwriting, he was wide open to helpful hints. But one thing he wasn't going to tamper with was the character of Sailor. He knew his man and felt confident that in the character of this gritty hell-for-leather little "bloodie" was the gold of the play. A once-great actor named Dominici auditioned for the part, much too old, a little too heavy, but somehow he, too, understood the stuff of Sailor. During the audition, Koner whispered to the author, "Let's get that drunken has-been out of here."

"No," said Shortner. "I want him." And he got him. "Why were you so good at that final soliloquy?" Shortner asked the shambling, wasted, yet still-brilliant performer. "Because my cousin just died," he said. Shortner felt he understood.

As the opening night drew near, Shortner wondered about Marse's motives. Why was he doing all this? Had it all begun with *Shorties from Shortner?* That seemed incredible. Perhaps Marse wanted to indulge himself in a sheer exercise in power, to demonstrate that he was God in the theater, capable of taking any piece of garbage and pronouncing it a hit. But surely he was already aware of his vast influence, although he had coyly denied it in a few interviews, giving as an example a play that had run thirty performances without his approval. Had he nursed some marginally sexual childhood attraction for Shortner, watching him secretly and with lust as he had run the quarter mile in a sweatsuit? Or perhaps it was a grudge. Stolid and joyless as a youngster, Marse might have resented Shortner's seemingly easygoing, carefree manner and what may have appeared to be a way with the girls. In that case, he was probably building up Shortner so that he could humiliate him with a two-fisted slam at the play. Worse yet, he might not even show up at all, sending the paper's second-string drama critic in his place. Two days before the opening, Shortner was thinking along these lines when a telegram arrived from Marse:

DON'T WORRY ABOUT A THING

On opening night, in violation of his usual last-second arrival style, Marse turned up twenty minutes before curtain time, giving first-nighters a chance to point at him and make whispered comments. When the play began, Shortner, as if it were expected, began to pace up and down in the rear of the theater, then caught himself and stopped. Why was he bothering to pace? He might as well go out and start the victory dinner at the second-rate French restaurant Koner had rented for old times' sake. Instead, he concentrated on the play, keeping an eye on Sailor, his favorite character in all theater, even though he had written him. He cursed himself for ever doubting Dominici's brilliance—which he had when the first rehearsals went poorly and he had begun to think that the fellow had faked him out in the audition. The decision had been to let Sailor die at the end of the play, going the noncommercial route. As if it made any difference. Still, it was Shortner's favorite moment. Sailor's girl, the bums gathered round, lights from the plasma bottles dancing and then funneling every eye in the theater toward Sailor's tears, and then the animal snarl in his voice as he comes up with the final ounce and dies. Shortner wept. But then he'd wept through all the rehearsals, too. No one could teach Shortner anything about Sailor, but Marse, in his rave notice, drew parallels between the blood being drawn out of Sailor's veins and the strength that was seeping out of America. The fight to save the old-timer, Cactus, was a struggle to arrest the decline of pure frontier values, ones that had infused the country with moral fiber. Shortner rejected some of these notions and bought a few. All were brilliantly expressed. The show was a solid hit. The other reviews were mixed. One called *King of the Bloodies* a "bloody bore," another hailed Gabe Shortner as a direct lineal descendant of Twain, O'Neill and Miller. If there had ever been any doubt of the power of Marse and his newspaper, the next day's line around the block for tickets settled the argument.

Marse wired his congratulations, a silly move, it seemed to Shortner. Ducking interviews and film offers, Shortner found his only real pleasure came from slipping into the theater each night to see his play again. If playwrights traditionally lost interest in their work once it was off and running, then Shortner was a new breed. He loved his play more each time he saw it, and never could get enough of certain moments—Sailor's first jaunty, grizzled appearance at the flophouse, the reunion of Sailor and his hooker girl friend (who incidentally had offered herself to Shortner backstage when the reviews came in), the sharing of a cup of ketchup soup by Sailor and his ravaged old friend Cactus to bring down the first-act curtain. Each night, the audience thundered its applause at the end of the play, Shortner roaring along with them. But did they really love that fierce, indomitable King of the Bloodies or was it Marse and his powerful newspaper leading them by the nose? One night, when the show was over, and Shortner had hugged Dominici for the thirtieth time, ignoring the alcohol on his breath, he made his way to Marse's newspaper office, there to find the drama critic in a huddled conference with one of the school reunion district attorneys. God only knows what deals they're cooking up, he thought to himself.

"It was wonderful," said Marse, who didn't seem overly surprised to see his old school chum.

"You said that in your telegram," said Shortner.

"I hear your play is about blood," said the D.A. "That ought to be right up my alley."

"It's about more than that," said Marse. "It's the first decent statement about these values of ours and why they've become so goddamned corroded."

"You said that in your review," said Shortner.

"Maybe I'll take it in," said the D.A.

"I'll set it up," said Marse.

"Except that right now I'm going sailing for the weekend."

"Why did you do this to me?" said Shortner when the D.A. had gone. He caught himself with his hands at his sides in a pleading style, a theatrical move he realized he had probably gotten from Dominici.

"Do what?" asked Marse. "Get you to write a play? Have it turn out to be great? Then make sure it's a hit?"

"There's something you don't understand," said Shortner. "I love my play. Do you have any idea of the way I feel when that cocky little bastard struts out on stage? And then they take the last ounce of blood out of his veins? And I'm sitting in the audience knowing that I made the guy up?"

"I love him, too," said Marse. "As much as you do. That little son of a bitch is America's last gasp."

"First of all, he's not America's last gasp and he never will be. He's a little guy who can keep coming up with blood until there's none left."

"He can be both."

"He can't be both. Second of all, how do I know the play is good?"

"You read what I said."

"Bullshit. You said you were going to say it."

"How about the audience," said Marse. "Did they say they were going to love it, too?"

"Maybe they're following your lead."

"Believe me, I'm not that powerful. Powerful yes, but not that powerful.

"Listen, Gabe," said Marse, taking off his glasses and rubbing tired eyes. "I'll say it once more. Realism, schmealism, call it what you will, it's an extraordinary piece of work. I'm going back to see it again in six months—I do this— but it's my view that it will stand up, who knows, maybe for another twenty years. I don't know what chemistry it comes out of, how it happened, but what you've got is a small miracle up there on stage, the most accurate poetic representation—and I know you hate this kind of thing— of America at the crossroads anyone has come up with in a decade. Now that's the way I see it, and it's my last word on the subject."

"Okay," said Shortner, "I'll let that stand. Now here's *my* last word." With that, he leaned across the desk and grabbed Marse by the throat, holding him immobilized with the use of two thumbs at the Adam's apple, a trick he had learned at officer's training school during the Korean War. "I'm writing another play. I have a glimmer of an idea, but what it's about is none of yours or anyone else's goddamned business. The piece ought to take me six weeks or so to finish, maybe ten with rewrites. I can't quite figure out one plot turn in the second act.

"But listen to this last part carefully," he said, tightening the thumb pressure. "If you so much as come within ten miles of me or my play, if you say one word about it to anyone, if you even *think* about it and most of all, when it's on the stage, if you *dare* to love it, I swear to Christ I'll kill you with my bare hands."

—1971.

# The
# Scientist

**H**AD THE CEREMONY BEEN SCHEDULED for Warsaw or New Delhi, he would have flown to either city immediately and without question; the very distance, the exotic setting, would have given a certain weight to the award. But many of the delegates were Europeans, anxious themselves to make a trip abroad, and there had been a decision to take the proceedings, almost literally, to Granville's doorstep; he was happy it had worked out that way. He would be able to continue his routine, which he now prized above all else in life.

Upon taking his stool at the luncheonette, he was given his tea almost immediately; there was no need to place an order. Granville was familiar with most of the town's residents, at least those who milled about at the noon hour, yet the woman who eased her way past his stool was new to him. Granville looked at her, not quite with alarm, but as though she were an animal he had caught intruding upon a small, carefully tended garden. As she worked her way past Granville, she clutched at his arm with what seemed to be an iron tentacle and it occurred to him that she was probably older than any person he had ever seen in the town. Her skin was dark and folded like an old, forgotten memo, and her eyes had a wild, chicken-like pop to them. It did not surprise him that she began to speak to him and it surprised him even less that the talk centered on the importance of staying spry and alert; also, her feeling that it was wrong to put old people to death, no matter what the circumstances. He listened with some interest, yet there was a curtain between them; he could get no more involved than if he were a journalist doing an interview. At most, she was twenty-five years his senior; yet this talk about "alertness" had nothing to do with Granville. Old Age,

Death, Alertness—he had not yet gotten around to thinking about them. He would take care of them "later." Once, as a much younger man, he had gotten an unguarded look at his reflection in the mirror of a tennis-club locker room and seen a new and somewhat slack conformation around his buttocks—the first significant change he had noticed in his body. It had bothered him at the time and then he had simply turned it out of his mind. The old woman beside him said that her grandchildren were quite proud of her and that when anyone asked how she was feeling she would sing *Glory, Glory, Hallelujah* to them. Granville enjoyed talking to her. But he did not really hear her. She was a prop, a background sound, a decoration for his daily routine.

It was flattering to think that men from as far away as the Soviet Union not only knew of his work but had traveled all this distance to honor him. His achievement had been legitimate, and yet Granville knew that in a sense he had been "playing over his head." As a young athlete many years before, he had had a similar experience; an average shooter, he had begun, during one basketball game, to score points from all over the court, almost involuntarily, each of his shots mysteriously guided through the hoop the instant he released the ball. Many years later, he had had one such day in his laboratory, a sudden breakthrough, for a few hours his mind yawning untypically, gaping wide; like an insane man he had clutched at the chance, working with demented fury, time counting for nothing, grabbing at the bait, catching enough of it, holding on and then settling back in exhaustion with his prize. The award had been earned and yet Granville knew that he had been responsible for "helping things along" ever so slightly. He was outwardly bumbling, absentminded, somewhat dissociated—yet it was a practiced style, and there was very clearly another side to Granville, one that saw to it he was taken care of. A key man on the committee was Krulski, a Pole. He had been on the East Coast several years before, an almost painfully dour, monotonous-looking man. Granville had invited the Pole to spend the weekend at his country home. Even as he performed this "simple act of kindness" to a lonely man, Granville was aware of its potential use to him. Then, too, Granville's very appearance—easy, comfortable, reassuring—must have helped him enormously. For so many years, he had been the complete opposite of these qualities; he'd been unstable, suspicious, somewhat paranoid. And yet, in a curious way, he had gradually changed and come closer to being what he appeared to be—as though he'd been forced to catch up with his physical image.

Granville paid the check, tipped his hat to the old woman and thought suddenly of his mother who had called early that morning just in case he'd gotten his dates mixed up and forgotten about the award luncheon. She had had a lingering cough, cold, slate-like, and he wondered if she was ever going to lose it. Through the many years of his married life, he had gotten almost completely away from her, but his wife's death had marked the end of his Liberation. Though he vowed it would never happen, in an almost sly manner he had gotten closer to his mother than ever before. He told himself they were on an entirely new basis, however.

He took the steps of the Town Hall briskly, very much aware of how vigorous he must have seemed to anyone watching. There were times, after sucking at his pipe for many hours, that he could not really get to the top of an honest breath, but he could not imagine reaching a stage in which he would be unable to dash up the Town Hall steps. His picture had been posted in the alcove and he was pleased to see that an open-shirted one had been cho-sen—one that made him seem both rugged and distinguished. He smiled at the receptionist and then thought of his mother's cough and wondered whether he should not schedule dinner with her for the following evening. It occurred to him that there might not be that many opportunities left. And then, still looking at his picture in the alcove, he imagined himself getting the news of his mother's death and putting his "plan" into action; he would drive immediately to an old resort in the Pennsylvania mountains where she had taken him so often as a boy— and sit at a bar and order a whiskey and think about her in the flush of her youth, and talk to the bartender and cry a little—and in that way honor her memory. He was not sure the resort still existed, but even if it had been turned into a dance hall or a skating rink, it would serve. He had been over the "plan" many times in his mind and was fairly certain he would follow it when the time came.

The Pole was the first to greet him at the Reception Hall. Their handshake was warm, yet broken off quickly, as though each of them feared that too much warmth might be observed and interpreted incorrectly. Granville said hello to many of the others and then took a short stroll with Krulski, both men walking with heads bowed slightly, arms locked behind their backs; it was a manner Granville had quickly adopted after his first international conference, one that came so naturally to him now he would never have considered it an affectation. They spoke English, coming back again and again—as they had that weekend— to such words as "humanity" and "mankind." It was politely fraudulent talk; Granville might have been uttering alien sounds in a Buddhist temple. Yet without the nuances of a common language, it was as close to communication as they were going to get. For a moment, as they stood on the terrace, Granville noticed that the Pole bore an almost nervous resemblance to his late uncle George. When Granville's mother was young and fatherless, according to her stories, it was always her brother George who had protected her, made sure she was warm at night, stole to get her dresses. Perhaps Granville had been kind to the Pole for more complicated reasons than he suspected.

There had been a time when meetings and luncheons did not bore him so much as frighten him, when he was happy to get them over with as soon as possible. He wanted this one to stretch on indefinitely and was a little sorry when the delegates were finally beckoned to the table. It felt comfortable sitting down with these people, some of them men of considerable achievement, all of them there to honor him. During the morning call, his mother, when she had been able to still her cough, had made the award seem even more important than it was. Even when he had broken off from her, through all the years of his marriage, he had defended her enormous gift of enthusiasm. He could not comprehend what it would be like to accomplish something in life and not have her there to exult, to be bowled over in her special way.

Considering the importance of the talk, he had thought of reading from a prepared text, but then realized there was little need for that. He thought briefly of his graduation, when he had gotten no further than the opening line of a memorized speech and had been gripped by a sudden rush of terror and forced to sit down in humiliation. It was terribly remote. It might have happened to another person, in another life. He was in command now. He owned his thoughts. They were as much a part of him as the brisk little trot he used for the Town Hall steps.

Once introduced, he took his time getting to his feet and for a moment stood at the dais without speaking a word. He listened to the delegates applaud with genuine fervor; their affection for him was warming—a cloak might have been placed about his shoulders.

"How remarkable," he began, finally, his voice rich, firm,

"that lodged in the flesh of mankind there exists a mysterious potential for scientific mommy that...." He could not be certain, of course, that he had actually uttered the word; it might have been a loose echo floating idly across his brain. He began again: "How remarkable that lodged..." but then he could no longer control himself and it spilled out of him in such a powerful mixing torrent of grief and loss that only the earth itself, deserted suddenly by a massive body of water, could ever have known. "Oh mommy," he said. "Oh mommy, mommy, mommy, don't die....Oh mommy, mom, mommy, mom, mommy, mom, mom...."

—1967.

# The Adventurer

SUDDENLY, GALLAGHER HAD NOTHING TO complain about. He had written a hit play; money poured in. He wanted a house; he had a house. He wanted a boat; a boat was his. His sons, formerly brooding, now smiled on him. After two years of marriage, his second wife looked at him as if he were a dish of ice cream. It was all he could do to fend off happiness.

One morning, he told his wife, "Christy, remember those sudden trips I used to take, just pick a place on the map—Panama City; French Lick, Indiana—take off and go? Remember how replenishing they were? Why don't I do that again?"

"I think you should. I've got plenty to do and I wouldn't mind being alone for a while."

The response, had it come from another woman, would have been menacing. But this was the good-natured Christy.

So off Gallagher went to sunny Florida, the choice not quite that random. In the corner of his mind was an almost perfect blonde—her hair did frizz in the rain—he had met at a bar, probably too many months before. After one quick look, he assumed she was beyond his reach. She was tall, coltish, tailor-made for preppies. But she had been charmed by his work in the theater. She tended bar; as she reached for Scotch bottles, her movements were balletic, unquestionably aimed at Gallagher. They had some coffee; she was an actress and a friend of judges. At her apartment, they wrestled on the rug. Calls came in from the judges. Behind a curtain, a roommate who paid most of the rent slept fitfully. So the deed remained undone. They had another date. Gallagher got to second base with her, then trotted off the field to go into rehearsals. She left for Lauderdale. Now, with a hit under his belt, Gallagher flew South to bat himself home.

With the greatest of ease, he tracked her down. He checked at one bar, was steered to another, the second trimmed with coconuts and tom-toms. Sleepy bearded fellows, vaguely nautical, roamed about. The jukebox was lively, up to date. A sign said, NO SAD STORIES. She had a rich tan and wore cut-off blue jeans. If possible, her legs had improved. She ignored him; he ignored her back. Then she summoned him to a corner table, reserved for the help. "I had to be careful," she said. "Half the guys are cops."

"What's that got to do with me?"

She chuckled, as if catching on to a sly remark. She was no longer involved with judges. Indeed, she had gone the other way and was now an intimate of heavies. Her boyfriend was Schoenfeld—in the immediate area, heaviest of all.

"Oh, well," said Gallagher, cashing in his chips. "I was just passing through and thought I'd say hello."

"Don't go," she said, catching his wrist. "Direct me. I like to be told what to do."

"Maybe we could hang out together, you, me, and Schoenfeld."

"Good," she said. She kicked her legs up on the table, lit a cigaret.

"One of the judges just wanted me to take showers with him," she said.

Gallagher took note of the sudden swerve in her logic— but it was a nice tidbit.

He checked into a handsome motel that appeared to be screamingly expensive but turned out to be dirt-cheap. One thing about having money, he said to himself, you can't seem to get rid of any.

He ordered up some clams on the half shell to keep his weight down, took a nap—and in the early evening, headed back to the bar. She was still there, whirling about with a drink tray. She worked long, fierce hours.

"He's over there," she said, directing him to a fellow with a spreading waist and a heavily pouched face. Schoenfeld wore a blazer and an unlaundered shirt, as if he had started to dress nicely, then said the hell with it.

"You look around the same age as me," he said to Gallagher. "I'm forty-six. How old would you say I was?"

"A little younger."

"That's what I say," he said, as if pleased, finally, to have an ally. "I was supposed to drive out to see my wife, but I've been up for five days. You don't think I should drive in this condition, do you?"

"No, I don't."

Schoenfeld appraised him through his pouched eyes, then said, "Come on inside, I'll fix you up."

Gallagher followed him past the jukebox and a bank of electronic games into the men's room. They went into the single stall, where Schoenfeld fed him generous amounts of medium-grade coke. Laughing Latins peered in at them.

"The traffic's a little heavy in here," said Gallagher.

"They're gonna fuck with me?" said Schoenfeld, raising an eyebrow. "Schoenfeld?"

They walked back to the bar. Gallagher was supposed to feel high, but he didn't. Schoenfeld patted the blonde girl on the head, then quickly joined Gallagher.

"The thing about starting a guy off on coke is then you have to continue him all night. But don't worry, I'll take care of you."

"Let me give you some money," said Gallagher.

"Schoenfeld?" he said.

A tall man with a quietly powerful body came into the

bar. He wore steel-rimmed glasses and had a short and truly dreadful haircut.

"Very heavy guy," said Schoenfeld, poking Gallagher softly. "His name is Shithead, but only if you're intimate. Otherwise, it's Ralph."

"Ralph is fine with me," said Gallagher.

"Hey, Shithead," Schoenfeld called out. "Say hello to Mr. Gallagher."

In the great tradition of seriously hard men, the fellow gave Gallagher a gentle handshake.

"Hi, Ralph," said Gallagher.

The big man looked around the bar. Some sleepy girls were now slumped over on their stools. They were there to join the sleepy bearded fellows.

"I used to put little girls up on my face before it came in," said the tall man. "Put 'em right up here," he said, demonstrating.

Schoenfeld gave him some coke, which he took to the men's room.

"Nicest guy in the world," said Schoenfeld, "and then he'll go off on you."

When the big fellow came back, a polka was playing on the jukebox. He lifted Gallagher off the ground and whirled him about the floor a few times like a rag doll. Gallagher, not your basic small man, thought of resisting, but having gotten some idea of the fellow's strength, decided it was a poor idea. He let himself go limp. The fellow put him down gently.

"I can do that," said Shithead, "because I think I read something of yours once."

"Let's hit some after-hours places," said Schoenfeld.

"So early?" asked Gallagher.

"They're nice now," said Schoenfeld.

Gallagher touched base with the blonde girl. "Maybe I'll

catch up with you later," he said.

"I'd like that," she said. Schoenfeld gave her a wave. She waved back and shook her head sadly. "All his girl friends leave him," she said.

They got into Shithead's pickup truck, which was equipped with powerful bumpers, and drove out to the highway.

Schoenfeld seemed worried about his wife. "Drive in my condition, I'd probably never make it," he said.

Shithead drove off the highway onto the service road a few times to ram some parked cars in their driveways.

"That's the type of thing I do," he said.

They stopped at a roadside place. The man at the door looked around nervously before admitting them, though there seemed to be no one else in view for miles around.

Gallagher and Shithead took seats at a bar while Schoenfeld had a hot discussion with a young fellow in a ruffled shirt who seemed to be in charge. The place was modest— it featured a spotless dance floor that appeared never to have been used and a lazy blackjack game in the rear. A trio of women Gallagher took to be hookers sat at one end of the bar. No one seemed to be having any fun. Schoenfeld and the man in the ruffled shirt took turns jabbing at each other's chests, then hugged each other, after which Schoenfeld joined them at the bar.

"They're very careful who they let in here," he said to Gallagher. "They had been briefed on Shithead, but I had trouble when it came to you. Anyway, you're in. You packin'?"

"No," said Gallagher.

"Everybody else is," said Schoenfeld, "but don't worry, you're with me."

A thin, pretty hooker dropped her compact on the floor. When she stooped to pick it up, she looked like a young mother straightening up a playroom. Shithead signaled to her and she followed him to the back area.

Schoenfeld fed Gallagher another taste of the medium-grade coke and said, "*You* get something good, you tell me. *I* get something good, I tell you."

"I doubt that I'll get anything good," said Gallagher. "But if I do, I will."

Gallagher went over to play some blackjack. The dealer handed him an eighteen, dealt himself one, too, and took Gallagher's money.

"Wasn't that a push?" asked Gallagher.

"We don't obey that," said the dealer.

He played a few more hands to be sociable, then returned to the bar.

"How'd you do?" asked Schoenfeld, yawning.

"They take pretty good care of themselves around here."

"Well, don't you worry," said Schoenfeld. "You're with me."

Shithead returned from the back section and had a whispered consultation with Schoenfeld. It looked as if they were exchanging stock tips.

"We got a problem," said Schoenfeld. "Shithead here just tied up a hooker in the ladies' room and left her there. When they find her, they'll be pissed."

"Shouldn't we leave?" asked Gallagher.

"Before I finish my drink?" said Schoenfeld.

He sipped his beer and dozed off at the bar. When the owner was summoned to the ladies' room, Shithead grabbed Schoenfeld and shook him awake. They followed Shithead out to the pickup. He gunned the motor and tore off down the highway, hunched over in the excited style of a wheelman, but no one appeared to be following them. He slowed down and they drove easily beneath a cheery Southern moon.

"I've got to tow some Arabs out of a dune," said Shithead. "I'm gonna charge them three hundred dollars. What do you think?"

"I think you'll get it," said Gallagher.

"If they object, I'll cold-cock them."

"Maybe I ought to go back to my wife," said Schoenfeld. "Even in this condition. When I spoke to her this morning, she said, 'Drive back or that's the marriage!' What do you think?"

"If she put it that way," said Gallagher.

"That's what I think. Shithead, drop me off."

His car was parked in someone's driveway. It was a Pontiac that looked as tired as he did.

"Call me," he said to Gallagher, as he got out of the pickup. He shook his head in disappointment. "Jesus Christ, you never call me."

"I just met you," said Gallagher.

"Well, don't be no stranger."

Shithead drove Gallagher back to the bar. He appeared to want to say something but seemed nervous about it. Finally, he said, "Maybe you ought to write my story. I used to beat up Gerry Cooney."

"He's vicious," said Gallagher.

"Not with me, he isn't." He kissed Gallagher full on the mouth, then dropped him off at the bar. Gallagher wiped off his mouth and went inside to see the blonde girl. The place was much livelier than the after-hours club.

"How did you do with my friends?" she asked.

"It's a long story," he said. "The truth is, I came down here to see you."

"What about my boyfriend?"

"We won't let him in on it."

"I don't know," she said. "We usually share things. Be forceful."

"Get your ass over to my place as soon as you finish up."

"You're on," she said, twirling around to serve a customer. Twirling back, she asked, "You a spanker?"

"It's not high on my list," said Gallagher.

"I like it," she said, "as long as it doesn't escalate."

She wore high heels and a cream-colored skirt and looked as if she were about to have lunch at the Plaza. He didn't understand the need for all the formality, but he was thrilled about the skirt.

"I could spend a month just arranging and rearranging it," he said.

"It would be cheaper than a summer in the Hamptons," she said. She hadn't budged from the doorway. "Do you want me to stand over here for a while and look shy?" she asked.

"I don't really require that," he said. They kissed for a while and then undressed. She went to great lengths to see to it that her clothes were folded meticulously.

"I wanted to follow up in New York," he said, amazed by her body, "but I got derailed."

"Oh, that's all right," she said. "I had the judges then anyway.

"Now," she said, rubbing her hands briskly, "were there any special things that you wanted?"

"Let's just see what happens," he said. They made love for a while. She was pretty skillful and he told her so. "How old did you say you were?" he asked.

"Twenty-four," she said, "but you're giving me excellent guidelines."

"Now," she said later, sitting up, brushing her hair, "how does your dream of a golden goddess hold up?"

"Just fine," he said, but he wasn't sure he meant it.

"You've helped me in a thousand different ways," she

said. "I wonder if you would take this eighth up to my girl friend in New York." She handed him a glassine packet of cocaine. "I'm behind in the rent."

Again, he was aware of a break in her logic, but he said he would take care of it. They had a few beers on the porch. "Remember," she said, putting on her heels. "Call me wherever you are, I'll meet you halfway." She left. Everyone wants me to call them, he said to himself. He rang up Christy.

"How's it going?" she asked. "You replenished yet?"

"I'm getting there," he said.

"I miss you and I love you."

"Love you, too, babe."

He left the next morning and headed for the airport. This was his first try at carrying drugs. He got his own body through without a hitch, then waited for his valise. "I was in San Ysidro a couple of years ago," he said to a disinterested female attendant. He thought she might be an American Indian. "Everyone was using surfboards to carry stuff in. What's the trend these days?"

"Wise guys," said a short, stocky man nearby. He flashed a badge and told Gallagher to empty his pockets. The packet slid out of a leather cigar case along with two fresh Havanas. The agent confiscated the packet, then held up one of the cigars and took an imaginary puff. "These any good?" he asked.

"Those are *my* cigars," said Gallagher, idiotically, and flew at him.

The agent, Feld, a nimble transplant from crowded Queens, did a side step and trailed a leg. It hooked the charging Gallagher and sent him up in the air. He actually enjoyed the sensation until he landed. The break sounded as if someone had stomped on a poorly wrapped package. Feld handcuffed him, sat him in the grated rear of a squad car and drove him to a doctor in a nearby shopping center. Later, his shoulder mounted importantly in a cast, he followed Feld across the parking lot to the squad.

On a nearby loading platform, Schoenfeld awaited him, clean-shaven, amazingly refreshed. "I heard what you did," he said. "When they're finished with you, then I start in." Behind him, Shithead kicked at the dirt, embarrassed.

A car drove up, carrying the thin hooker and the after-hours man, in a fresh ruffled shirt. He squinted one eye, aimed a finger at Gallagher and went, "*Bing.*"

Gallagher followed the agent into the squad. A brush-fire of pain lit up his genitals. He imagined three kinds of V.D., only one of them a pushover. He did some quick calculations: Even with a clean slate and impressive character references, he faced a minimum of three to seven in the can.

"I don't understand you," said Feld, starting up the squad. "You don't seem like the type. And I understand you had a big success up East."

Gallagher sighed, stretched out his legs. The seat was wet, as though a frozen turkey had been there before him. In the distance, Schoenfeld bared his teeth and raised a fist.

"I know what you mean," he said to the agent. "But I seemed to have a need to complicate my life a little."

—1981.

# An Ironic
# Yetta Montana

**T**HIS IS A STORY ABOUT the one time I outfoxed Hollywood. Open on me arriving at the Pierre Hotel for a script conference with Sandra Moxie, a short, feisty, singer slash actress with a brash, almost harassing style and the uncanny ability to turn around on a dime and become quite touching. Or at least *most* people felt she had that ability. In her recent appearances, I myself had felt that you could see the machinery, that she was telegraphing her touching stuff with the result that it wasn't all that touching. But let that pass. For the moment, let's just say that she was touching enough to get the job done.

As a singer, Moxie had built up a strong following in Key West and Marin County and had received critical plaudits for a film cameo in which she had hit a leering computer programmer over the head with a jar of peanuts and then casually spun around and sung a ballad from a bar stool. The plaudits, for the most part, were foreign plaudits—awards she had to share with Dolly Parton—but there was no question that her alternately harsh and vulnerable style was effective on film. Inevitably, a search began for a property that would take full advantage of the special Moxie capabilities. It was in this context that I was hired by an independent film producer to do the true story of Yetta Montana, the daughter of an East Coast dry-goods salesman, who went west to become a honky-tonk bar owner and the only woman to stake out a fortune in the Klondike Gold Rush of 1897. Amazingly, Montana was still alive, albeit hanging on by her thumbs, and I got to interview her in a condominium in Sarasota. She went in and out on me, memorywise, but for those moments when she was in the game, she was surprisingly lucid. (I should probably add that the celebrated Montana bosom was also—I'm not

sure *intact* is the word—very much in the picture.) She
wore a replica of her diamond-studded rotary drill around
her neck and she had kept some remarkably well-
preserved diaries, along with photographs of her hanging
out with panhandlers on the Klondike River. She was kind
enough to let me borrow these materials and I assured her
I would get them back to her in good condition. Admittedly, it was difficult to get a fix on Montana and what her
gold-field style might have been like. Nonetheless, I did
some fancy extrapolating, took a quick free-form run at
the story and sent the result to Sandra Moxie, underlining
the fact that it was a *first draft*. Shortly thereafter, I heard
she had "a few reservations" (the most ominous phrase in
the film biz) but wanted to see me all the same. I had heard
she was given to tantrums and violent swings of mood, but
I took it as a matter of course that, although some gifted
people could be difficult, they tended to meet you on your
own terms if you behaved in a firm and professional manner.

In person, Moxie was shorter than she appeared on-
screen (where she came across pretty short) but not in the
least bit feisty. At least in the early innings. She wore a
shapeless garment, a cross between a housedress and a
dashiki, and struck me as the kind of person who allowed
herself to fall apart for a while and then went on crash
programs to get in shape. She didn't appear to be on one
of those programs at the moment. She was courteous,
speaking in a low, evenly modulated voice; her style, if
anything, was on the plaintive and even borderline heartbroken side.

"I heard you weren't entirely pleased with the script," I
said, throwing out a signal that I was easy and flexible in
the work relationship and certainly not one of those people
who fought you tooth and nail for every semicolon.

"That's a fair summation," she said. And then, in a

wounded heartbroken rush, she added: "Truthfully, I don't see Yetta Montana. The Yetta I've been expecting is brash, feisty, up one minute, down the next, laughing, crying, wounded, depressed, but no matter what the circumstances, always punching and kicking back at the world—every inch a woman.

"*This* person," she said, hitting my script, "is a wimp. I wouldn't play her if they gave me an Oscar in advance."

Her outburst put me on the defensive. Fortunately, after long years as a screenwriter I had learned to be at ease in that posture.

"Kicking? Punching? Who told you Yetta was like that?"

"Everyone," she said. "Why do you think I wanted to do the part!"

I let the "wanted" go for the moment.

"Well, I actually met the woman," I said. "And she isn't at all like that. She has some drive—you don't beat out forty thousand rival prospectors if you're a lox—but I didn't see any kicking and punching. Actually, it's the *other* colors that come through. She's soft, whimsical, a little flirtatious...."

"How old is she now?" asked Moxie.

"Old," I said, caught. "Pretty damned old. But I assure you people don't change that much. The blueprint is still there."

"When McClintock attacks her girl friend, why doesn't she hit him right over the head?"

"She arranges to have his mule team scattered. That's not exactly Gandhi-like resistance."

"*Arranges,*" she said, with a smirk. "Got a big, strong man to do it for her. That's exactly my point."

She sat down and folded her arms.

"I'm not playing a wimp."

Well, I'd been around the horn a few times with female stars. The-entire-script-is-a-turkey. I-wouldn't-play-the-part-if-you-tripled-the-salary. Poke around a bit and you find out the trouble is: a) she doesn't appear early enough, b) she doesn't want to wear toreador pants and c) the side-kick has a few good one-liners. In other words, Mickey Mouse.

"Why don't we just dig in," I suggested, "scene by scene and see if we can't spot the areas you're objecting to. "For example," I said, confident my first few pages were un-assailable, "what do you think of the opening?"

"It's a cliché."

"Hold it," I said. "Time out right there. A scene with a *gay* rail-splitter is a cliché? How many scenes have you looked at with gay rail-splitters?"

"Oh, for God's sake," she said, as if I were a hopeless case. "Don't you even go to the movies?"

Well, the truth is, I don't go to the movies that often. I go in streaks, but then, there are long periods when I don't go—and although I have grave doubts about this—maybe there was some kind of trend I had missed. We moved to the second scene, which, in truth, even I wasn't too crazy about so I couldn't blame her for being unenthusiastic. I had dummied up a sentimental farewell confrontation be-tween the teenage Yetta and her father—just before she heads west—in which he warns her not to equate a troy ounce of gold with a troy ounce of happiness. Cast the right actors and you're in business. But if you can't envision a Rod Steiger in the role (with Steiger it flies right off the page), I have to admit it kind of lays there. Unfortunately, her reaction to the scene set the tone for the next twenty minutes or so, in which she halfheartedly conceded I had a usable minute here, another one there. At some point, she maneuvered herself over to the desk and came back holding a stack of papers, clutching them to her chest the way a schoolgirl might carry her first try at romantic poetry. A movie schoolgirl. She blushed a little and for a second she almost had me believing she was pretty.

"Do you mind looking at this?" she asked, handing the material to me. "When I got your script, I became panicky, so I dug into some turn-of-the-century newspapers and did a little work of my own. Bear in mind, I'm not a writer, but see what you think."

What I thought was that the work was not too shabby. Predictably, it got off the ground with a pretitle sequence in which Montana, new to the Klondike, outwardly shy and gullible, suddenly heaves a pan of unsifted gold dust in the face of a crass trail guide. To be fair about it, just because I could predict the resolution of the scene didn't mean that an audience would be able to. After that, the script kind of settled in, except that it *didn't* really settle in and therein lay its effectiveness. She used crazy discordant transitions that worked, just the way she did in her act. Cinematically, the technique was even more effective. *Bam* you're in Helena, *whop* you're in Forty-Mile, *klunk* you're aboard the S.S. *Excelsior* and *voom* you're back in the car, wondering where the movie went. Which wasn't all that bad. There weren't any layers, but so what. It's a god-damned entertainment. Let Fassbinder do layers. The best thing about it was that it was all *there* for me. Tone down the showbiz references, beef up the meeting with the aging Bat Masterson (adding a line or two to explain what the hell he was *doing* there), throw a line or two to Choppy Waters, Moxie's Cree sidekick, and that's it. Sign the script, mail it off and hunker down to audit the profit statements.

As I flipped through the last few pages, she leaned close and the celebrated Moxie bosom brushed against my ear. I pretended I hadn't noticed and she withdrew to a discreet distance, although what the word *discreet* is doing in this tome I'm not sure I can answer.

"You like it?" she asked, pleased in advance. Nobody ever said she didn't have delicate antennae.

"I do."

"Can I have a credit?"

"Nope."

We both laughed and decided it was as good a time as any to break for lunch. She opened a small refrigerator and took out some berries, melon slices and a few croissants, all of it left over from a breakfast with the Lorimar people. She asked me to bear with her—yes, the studio was tabbing her, but the frugal style was something she couldn't help. It was a carry-over from the years she'd worked in an all-night nail clinic while she was waiting for a break in show business. No doubt this would have been endearing to someone who wasn't crazed with hunger for a hot club sandwich the way I imagined only the Pierre could prepare one. While she warmed up the croissants, I riffled through the books on the shelves and was surprised at the quality of the selections. Normally, in my experience with hotels, it's the Gideon Bible, Taylor Caldwell if you're lucky, and out. But someone had stocked these shelves with Gide, Rilke, *Joseph and His Brothers*, not just Henry James but James's *letters*, for Christ's sake. I picked up a volume by an author I'd never heard of entitled *The Notebooks of Lotte Kastlemeir*, glanced at a few pages and became intrigued. Even allowing for the obvious debt to Mann and Nabokov, the style was instantly winning and unique. I asked Moxie if I could take it along.

"Do you know what this room costs?" she said, setting the food on the table. "Take a dozen."

We sat down to lunch and she asked me if I was married.

"No," I said. "I was, but I'm not."

"You live with someone?"

"Uh-huh."

"Yeah, and I can just see her. Probably a wimp."

To this day I still can't figure out why I was as upset as I was over that remark. Admittedly, it was sudden, unprovoked, major-league rude and anyone would have been upset. But dizzy spells? Strangulated rage? Pass-the-Gristede's-Shopping-Bag-I'm-Hyperventilating? And what happened to my famous above-the-battle posture in which I cluck my tongue and shake my head sadly, the one that really puts people away.

Was I stung because Kai-Yin really *was* a wimp? Actually, I'd never been with a woman who took care of me so totally. From the second I get up in the morning, it's feathery kisses, a bright and cheery smile and a scented cloth for the crust that forms over my eyes whenever we're at our place in Brooklyn Heights. After that, it's back massages, freshly laundered clothing, ingenious flower arrangements—the whole day is a parade of sensual delights. In the food department, all I have to do is *think* exotic, and she's out there with gimchee and a banana flambé. Kai-Yin is solicitous and caring, but does that mean she's a wimp? What happened to the whole Oriental tradition? Are we throwing that out? All right, for argument's sake, let's say she *is* a wimp. I've got a charming little Oriental wimp waiting for me in New Milford. Does that mean that the opposite of a wimp is short, feisty Sandra Moxie who can go from tough to vulnerable?

"Maybe we ought to go back to work?"

"Why don't you go out with Dustin Hoffman's ex-wife?"

Okay, why didn't I leave at *that* point? It's a fair question. I wasn't hired to be Kurt Waldheim. The money jumps to mind, but I'd been well taken care of on the first draft and if the studio said, "All right, bring in Hack Number Two," I'd already established that it was *my* notion, *my* characters and I'll see everybody at the Writer's Guild arbitration. The producer of the film was Norton Kranzler, an ancient "soft lefty" who had shielded blacklisted writers from his villa in Saint Paul de Vence. Was I staying because of my loyalty to Kranzler, a sick man whose voice could barely be heard over the phone and who hadn't had a hit since his brief partnership with Von Stroheim?

She was aware of my struggle—those street instincts left over from the all-night nail clinic. "I don't care if you quit," she said. But it was spoken with a surprising lack of bravado. "I took some development money from the studio. I'll just give it back."

"Anyone can quit," I said, wondering what had happened to the youth whose rapier-like cafeteria thrusts in the Bronx had virtually forced the yearbook editors to name him "The Oscar Wilde of William Howard Taft High School."

"Do you like working with me?" she asked, once again catching me off guard.

"Yes," I said. How could I not like working with her? She'd done the whole damned script for me.

"Do you like me?"

"I don't know how to answer questions like that."

She set the pages aside and kicked her legs up on the table.

"How much did they pay you for this job?"

I told her. It was ten grand more than I'd ever gotten before and I was a little proud of it.

"Jesus Christ," she said. "I know a film *student* in Santa Monica who gets a third of that. DON'T YOU EVER WRITE ME A SCRIPT LIKE THAT AGAIN!"

I didn't quit, didn't correct her grammar, didn't even toss her out the window. What I did do is thank her for the help, tell her I thought I could bring it much closer on the second shot and flipflop dissolved myself into the lobby. At the moment, I wasn't thinking wounded pride. All I knew was that I had a week's work in front of me and I was home. The second draft paid spit, but we're talking about *seven days*. Not even full-out days. Noon to around 3:30. With sandwiches brought in, I might even be able to knock it off in a weekend. And I'd have my first major credit. Even if they brought in two, three guys, there's no way they can bump me out of first position. And the picture was going to be big. Set aside my personal feelings about the woman—but Sandra Moxie in her first major role, wailing in the gold fields? Forget it, she's got to win something.

Anyway, there was no week and there was certainly no weekend. I had forgotten—there never is. The week turned into ten days which quietly became six weeks and by the time I got it back from the typist and bounced it off Kranzler (who maddeningly wanted some of Yetta's softness restored) I'd lost a season. Money-wise, unless the picture got made, I'd taken a beating.

I flew over to London to see Moxie, who was doing a record promotion there, and checked into the Dorchester, which had certainly changed since the last time I'd been abroad. A guy in a burnoose took me up to my room. When I called Moxie, someone who sounded like a girl friend said she was napping but that she would get back to me. I watched a little rugby on television—the only thing I could pick up—and then I got a call from Moxie's agent saying that she had changed her mind about the picture and didn't want to do it. Just like that. Nothing to do with me, but she'd taken something else. (A Western, I later found out, in which her sidekick is a gay rail-splitter.) Well, could I at least *speak* to her? No, that was out of the question. Contractually, she couldn't talk to me. I pointed out that I had flown a few miles for this meeting and that I'd already seen the Thames. A simple phone call would have saved me a lot of aggravation. He was sorry, but nothing could be done. The funny thing is, he really *was* sorry, in more ways than one. For a year, he had been pitching me as a client; I was there when he told a group at the Dome that he had absolutely no compunctions about mentioning my name in the same breath as Alvin Sargent's.

I was stunned, but I hung around the hotel figuring that as a human *being* she'd at least pick up the phone. No sad stories. I'd been paid for the work. But how do you get compensated for all that time with a tight stomach? For having a blockbuster dangled in front of you and then whisked away? I could have called her, of course, but that would have taken away a chance to feel sorry for myself and to take a look at my wonderful screenwriting career. Twelve years, fourteen scripts, and all I had to show for it was a shared credit on a Cadillac Western and an unreleased rock adaptation of *The Pit and the Pendulum.* I did have a blinking "go" on a horror flick but that was only if the German money held. Maybe it was time to call my own bluff and go up to Vermont and try a novel. I was sure Kai-Yin would give up her acting lessons with Stella Adler. How much could it cost to live up there? Why should I keep killing myself and always winding up with my feelings hurt? I was pretty stubborn about hanging around the hotel, but she never did call and I finally decided to pack it in. The studio was paying for the trip so I did stay in London for a few days. Did they expect me to cheerfully jump on the next plane? After getting my head handed to me? My stay didn't work out too well, and it's probably because my heart wasn't in it. I ate a lousy Chinese dinner, got my ring stolen by a hooker and wound up sitting in the Dorchester lobby with a Czech director who told me that he had just thrown a hundred pages of some guy's script in the fire, but that there were certain writers he'd always wanted to work with and I was one of them. I gambled a little at the 21 Club but even winning a few

shekels didn't cheer me up. So I decided the hell with it,
I'm gone.

It was on the plane back that the most amazing thing
happened. I reached into my briefcase for a last look at
the screenplay and came across the book I'd taken from
Moxie's suite at the Pierre on our first meeting. I started
to flip through it idly. At first, I was so depressed I could
barely focus on the print and then all of a sudden I was
practically bouncing up and down in my seat with excitement. It was all I could do to contain myself which was
important since there were a couple of ICM agents across
the aisle who were straining to get a look at what I was
reading. But what a find! It's a fictional first-person account of the life of an impoverished young beauty who
pulls herself out of the slums of Kitzbühl to become the
leading con woman in *fin de siècle* Vienna. Eventually she
pulls off a major swindle in which all of Central Europe's
*chocolatières* are brought to their knees. But talk about parts
for women. From the opening in which she's hauled out
of Gmunden Lake (in a failed suicide attempt) to the final
moment in which she icily rejects the marriage proposal
of the duke of Briganza (she may or may not be bearing
his child—you never find out and we may have to fix that),
the scenes come pouring out of the pages like a tidal wave.
The madcap affair with the great Schnitzler, the fire at
the Hairdressers League, the nude boar hunt with Krafft-
Ebing in Budapest—if there's anything that woman doesn't
do I'd like to know about it. I can just hear someone saying
"The kids won't buy it." Well, all I can do is turn their
attention to a hilarious little gem of a *schlag* fight with Mrs.
Mahler in Saint Stephen's Cathedral. If the kids don't go
for that, I'm leaving the business. Obviously, there's enough
material for three movies here, and yet, for all the dramatic
abundance, it's the tone that really puts it over the top, the

sly, deadpan way in which Kastlemeir justifies her outrageous behavior and almost has you believing she had no other choices in life. It's ironic, of course—actually, it's kind of an ironic Yetta Montana—but there's nothing weird about it. It's legit irony—the kind a mass audience can grasp. (There's no reason it won't hold its own in the South.) I don't know *who* you get to do the screenplay. Pinter? Bo Goldman? Maybe Pinter to get you started and come *in* with Goldman. The important thing is it's not going to be me. I'm finished busting my hump on that kind of work. This struck me as a perfect time to take my first shot as a producer. In any case, I didn't take my first comfortable breath until my agent searched out the property and found out it was in the public domain. There'd been a stage version written by a skiing instructor that ran three performances in Gstaad and we put a lock on that just in case.

So I'm sitting around with an extraordinary piece of material that cost me three cents and I can't help chuckling over the way it came into my hands—as a spinoff of my darkest moment in the business. Casting is no problem. We've got it with Streep's people and of course she'd be marvelous although truthfully, if she passes, I won't be heartbroken. Her price is out of sight and I can't help thinking she's a little severe for the role. Severe is okay, but only if it's combined with playful. I've screened all of her films and so far I don't see the playful. None of which matters since the piece is actor-proof. Life's too short to go with Dunaway, but you've got Hawn, Keaton, Fonda, even Shields if you want to wait a few years. Flatten out the rural thing and you might even slip through with Sally Field. Even Moxie, for Christ's sake, although I wouldn't think of it. I can't help wondering, though, about the way she would handle that thin line between severe and playful. But don't worry, I haven't sunk that low. I wouldn't have her in the picture if they gave me a dime on dollar one at the box office, which is ridiculous since not even Lucas gets that. I just pride myself on being able to look at these things with cold eyes.

—1981.

# The War Criminal

ONE DAY MESSINGER BROKE HIS rule about not going to local cocktail parties and found out his psychiatrist was an ex-Nazi. It was an evening that had been slightly off center from the beginning. Arriving early, he ordered two drinks from the bartender who served them up with a wink and said: "How's your wife's arse?" Messinger thought this was strange behavior on the part of the hired help and brought it to the attention of the host who said: "He's actually a cellist and he's all we could get." A little later, one of the guests put on a Western Union cap and went up and down the halls, in and out of each of the rooms, hollering: "Telegram for Phil Messinger, telegram for Phil Messinger." He tried to ignore the man, but soon all eyes were on him and he felt he had no choice but to walk up to the fellow and say: "All right, I'll take it."

The man, not really that drunk, said: "One dollar and fifteen cents, please," and Messinger went along, handing him the money.

"It's from the President," said the man, reading from a piece of paper. "It says:

GO HOME AND CHANGE YOUR UNDERWEAR.
IT HAS HOLES IN IT.


The host came up quickly behind Messinger and said: "Don't let him get to you. He's got some dull job in flexible packaging."

Searching for a safe haven, Messinger joined a group of women in the kitchen, one of whom was giving her views on interior design.

"When I walk into a room," she said, "I like it to say 'Howdy' to me."

Messinger surprised himself by saying: "And I like a room to keep its mouth shut."

He was evidently still smarting from the underwear telegram. The woman seemed to perspire suddenly. Toweling herself down with a dishrag, she said: "Oh, you're the one who goes to Doctor Newald. Do you mind about his being an ex-Nazi?"

Although it had been a strangely tilted evening, spilling over with bad behavior, Messinger believed the woman totally. Still, quite naturally, he resented her passing on the information in such a casual manner and said: "You know this for sure about Newald, is that it?"

"Yes."

"And you're just standing here at a party telling me about it?"

"Um hm."

"You're quite a sensitive person."

Although to the best of his knowledge he hadn't picked it for that reason, Messinger lived in an area that was heavily favored by psychiatrists as a place of residence. The streets were crammed with psychiatric homes; as a result, the community seemed to have an odd, quizzical tone to it. Arguments rarely raged, questions were answered in only the most tentative way and casual street chitchat was carried on in a warily relaxed manner. Strangers, passing on the street, seemed to do rapid-fire thumbnail sum-ups of one another. In the supermarket, bearded Jungians strolled the dessert aisle, pulling out all stops in their fantasized disrobing of the teenage checkout girls, at the same time smiling beatifically and congratulating themselves on their adjustment to the demands of everyday family life. One day Messinger saw a woman trip and fall against the out-of-town letter slot at the post office. A cool man in emergencies, he scooped her up and drove her to a nearby hospital. With blood pumping from her scalp, the woman held the torn cleavage of her dress together in a most feminine manner and said: "I guess I must have directed some of my aggressive tendencies toward myself." On still another occasion, Messinger stopped a poorly dressed Puerto Rican and asked him if he knew of anyone in the area who wanted to do floor shellacking for excellent pay. The man chuckled and said he could not be of any help. Later, Messinger was told the fellow was a neurologist, world renowned for his work on upper-class teens who wet their beds in defiance of wealth and privilege.

In a curious way, Messinger did not feel in the least bit put upon by the psychiatric currents in the air. A store window designer by trade, he felt his own status elevated by all the doctors in the area. Then, too, their presence seemed a protection against terrifying things happening to him and to his family. If indeed there were a calamity, he pictured the doctors gathering round it, analyzing it, somehow making it mute and removing its fangs. He was happy, nonetheless, that Newald lived many miles away and sympathized with patients in town who ran the daily risk of bumping into their analysts over a tuna and rye, or perhaps lying massage table to table with them at the local health club.

Messinger found himself curiously unaffected by the ex-Nazi disclosure and wondered, happily, if he had not become spiritually exhausted. Someone he admired a great deal was a young retired poet who sat each night at a bar in the city, a shawl wrapped around his neck, drinking Spanish brandy and playing solitaire. He seemed to do nothing else at all with his life and when Messinger asked a musician about him one night, he was told: "Victor's

spiritually exhausted." Messinger found this romantic and
attractive and felt a little sad about his own spirit which,
in its darkest moments, always struck him as remaining
peppy. Now, perhaps, it had caved in. He had been seeing
Dr. Newald for three years and was not clear on what stage
of treatment he was in. The visits had become mechanical,
like morning shaves. He knew only that he was a far different fellow from the one who—three years before—was
convinced he was about to be surgically unzipped from
head to toe, as if he were a duffel bag. And worried about
a tumor; although Messinger himself was a bundle of weak-
ness, he was convinced that the growth, ironically, would
be brawny and willful, the first tough thing about him.
One day, falling apart at the seams, he had pressed himself
against the glass of one of his window displays and considered marching through it. Then, thinking better of this
notion, he had walked into a building nearby which, as it
turned out, was the embassy of a fresh new African nation.
Messinger asked the receptionist if she knew of a psychiatrist; as if it were the most frequently asked question at
her desk, she referred him to Newald across the street. A
casual recommendation, but not necessarily a bad one.
Messinger seemed to receive all the major news of his life
in a casual manner. The night of his father's death, he had
been unable to get a good telephone connection to the
hospital; after asking him to redeposit his dime, it was the
operator who took over and told him his father was gone.
A bakery clerk had inadvertently told him his mother was
sleeping with a Pakistani and now, quite casually, it was an
interior designer who passed along the news of Newald's
Hitlerian background. He was angry at her, but not particularly at Newald.

Though he knew and cared little about the analytical
process, Messinger did have one firm view on the subject—

it mattered little to him whether the doctor was a sex pervert, a homicidal maniac, a nine-time loser in the divorce courts or a keeper of tarantulas—all that counted was the quality of what went on between him and his patient in the privacy of his office. On one occasion, Messinger's town was shaken by the news of a voyeuristic psychiatrist, out for a thrill, who had tripped on a building ledge and tumbled nine stories below to his death. It was on everyone's mind, yet so chilling were its implications to the psychiatrist-packed community that few dared speak of it. Without bothering to introduce the subject, Messinger leaned across his backyard fence one day and told a neighbor, "Yes, but if he came back from the dead tomorrow, I wouldn't hesitate to see him for treatment."

In one sense, Newald's Third Reich background fit neatly into Messinger's view and for the first two sessions after the news, almost smugly he failed to say a word about the perhaps gossipy revelation. In truth, just before the second visit, he did take a good look at Newald and try to imagine him in a jackbooted Wehrmacht uniform. Newald was a small pudgy man with slightly simian features who looked as though he might have been born on the Sino-Soviet border. Additionally, he spoke with a slightly tough-guy Lower East Side accent and it was difficult picturing him in uniform; after some effort, Messinger did manage to slip him into one. Still, he made no mention of the decorator's accusation; indeed, he took wide detours around any references that had the slightest inference of post-war guilt to them. Messinger had to admit nonetheless that it was in the air, not so much because he was one to go about in a festering—and profitless—rage over Nazi crimes, but more because it was there, something unspoken between them; he could not ignore it totally any more than he could overlook a splinter, no matter how microscopic in size. Before the third session, he found himself looking at Newald's office paintings, attractively troubled and dreamlike, and wondering whether they were not the work of young Germans of the new breed, embarking on their own road, petulant and snappish about references to their country's past. Midway along in this third session, Messinger struck pay dirt with a line of thinking about an uncle who'd always seemed to be innocent but now turned out to have an awful lot to do with blocking Messinger's development. Instead of barreling through to new insights, he suddenly veered off and said: "I heard at a party that you're an ex-Nazi." Newald said nothing. The sound of the air purifier seemed louder than before. After a few beats, almost as though the real reason he had stopped talking was to blow his nose, Messinger continued his previous monologue.

Evidently, Newald saw the accusation as being so ridiculous it did not even warrant comment. The following day, Messinger, relieved, had every intention of tunneling deeper into the strange influence of his uncle on his own bottled-up personality. But just as if a highway trooper had flagged him over to the side, he found himself kicking off the session by bringing up once again Newald's possible membership in the Nazi Party.

"Even if it's true, I like to think I'm tough enough to just sail right on with our relationship. But I *would* like to get it out on the table. Nine chances out of ten, it's cocktail-party gossip. I insulted the woman and she probably wanted to get back at me with something cute. Anyway, what's the deal? Yes or no, because I really think I'm on to something with my uncle."

Newald remained silent and Messinger, after a moment or so, said: "All right, I'll accept that," and with some difficulty continued, although he had become terribly aware of a pungent new smell in the office, appealing and disturbing at the same time. Had it been left over by the last patient? If she was dreamy, Messinger felt he would be able to lie back and enjoy it. If not, he wanted no part of it. Midway through the session, Messinger said he was a little disturbed by the smell.

"It's a new cologne I'm wearing," said Newald.

Messinger immediately leaped up from the couch, an extraordinary move considering he hadn't done it before in three years, and said: "You'll answer that, but you won't say anything about Nazis."

He sat on the couch, but did not lie down, holding his feet slightly above the rug as though there were alligators swimming about. Newald, totally visible now, seemed small and homely; he was guilty of a dozen fashion blunders and Messinger was able to see immediately the advantage of lying with his back to him.

"It's quite true, you know," said Newald.

"It is?" said Messinger, who hadn't counted on receiving the news in a face-to-face confrontation.

'We've never had any secrets up until now," said Newald in a gentle, bordering on the sweet, tone, "and I don't believe in having this one."

"Well, what's the deal," said Messinger, wanting to lie down again, but embarrassed about doing so, "a screw-up and when you found out what they were doing, you checked out immediately?"

"No," said Newald. "I must be honest with you. I suppose that I more or less knew what was going on and I didn't do anything about it. I just stayed."

"Christ," said Messinger. "There are probably dozens of guys like you in practice all over the country."

"Not dozens," said Newald, snatching more and more of the ground from beneath Messinger's feet. "A few."

Messinger suggested that Newald was probably in some piddling kind of administrative work and when the doctor assured him that this was so, he felt he had finally scored a point. Newald then told a somewhat routine story about his training and indoctrination, one that Messinger, a World War II and Hitler's-Rise-to-Power buff, found entirely familiar and not juiced up in the slightest by Newald's listless, formal way with an anecdote. Almost as though he were doing a routine civil service check, Messinger asked Newald if he had ever killed anyone.

"One," said Newald, holding up a finger. He said that he had been an orderly in a prisoner's hospital at the time and had been put in charge of an apparatus that was designed to keep serious post-surgery patients alive.

"There were some controls. A knob, particularly, that had to be turned regularly. At one point, I could not bring myself to turn it and, perhaps as a result, the man perished. He was old and feeble and probably would have died anyway, but I don't excuse myself. It was murder by negligence."

Consciously making a grave face—as if he were the doctor—Messinger asked if the man was a Jew.

"I don't know," said Newald. "He was a Nazi prisoner. He may have been a Polish officer. I must say that a fair and prudent guess would be that, yes, he was a Jew. It was not an issue as far as I was concerned. To my recollection, I remember being hypnotized by the power I had to grant life and death and found the temptation to kill him irresistible."

"So that's about it, eh?"

"That's about it," said Newald, softly, looking straight into Messinger's eyes. "I've repented, studied hard, spent more than twenty-five years trying to atone for my misdeed. Speaking quite truthfully, I suppose it's one reason why I've cultivated this Lower East Side accent of mine."

"I'm glad you brought that up," said Messinger. "I'd always wondered about it. But that's the whole story?"

"Every word."

"No gold fillings, no Jewish babies, nothing like that?"

"Nothing at all like that."

"I'm not going to go to another party and hear about a little death camp you ran on the side?"

"No, Mister Messinger."

"I guess my worst story for some reason is the Jewish boxer one. They got him to put on the gloves and then the German commander put on a pair, except that he kept a revolver in one of them. When the Jewish guy put his hands up to fight, the German shot him through the head. It's amazing that of all the horrors—and believe me, I've read about 'em all—that's the one that keeps haunting me."

"I've told you everything."

"Well, good," said Messinger, briskly snapping his legs up in front of him and glad to be back on the couch again. "Just so long as it's out in the open. I'd like to get back to my uncle. The thing I remember about him is that every time he came to our house, he always had his hands on mom's shoulders."

—1974.

# Marching
# Through Delaware

ONE NIGHT, DRIVING FROM WASHINGTON to New York, Valurian, for the first time in his life, passed through the state of Delaware, and felt a sweet and weakening sensation in his stomach when he realized that Carla Wilson lived nearby. All he would have to do is sweep off one of the highway exits; at most she would be half an hour away. Twenty-two years before, at a college in the West, he had loved her for a month; then, in what appeared to be a young and thoughtless way, she had shut the door abruptly in his face. Much later, he became fond of saying it was a valuable thing to have happen and that he was grateful to her for providing him with that lovely ache of rejection. But in truth, and particularly at the time, it was no picnic. He remembered her now as being thin-lipped and modest of bosom, but having long, playful legs and an agonizingly sexual way of getting down on floors in a perfect Indian squat. She had no control over her laugh; it was musical, slightly embarrassed and seemed to operate on machinery entirely separate from her. She had an extraordinary Eastern finishing-school accent, although to his knowledge she had attended no Eastern finishing school. She was an actress; he reviewed her plays for the local newspaper. Members of the drama group, some of whom had been in Pittsburgh repertory, referred to him as the "village idiot." Although she often did starring roles, the most he ever awarded her was a single line of faint praise. On one occasion, he said she handled the role of Desdemona "adequately." He was quietly insane about her; in his mind, the paltry mentions were a way of guarding against any nepotistic inclinations. It was a preposterous length to go to; she never complained or appeared to take notice of it.

Although he remembered quite sharply the night he got his walking papers, he had only disconnected, bedraggled recollections of time actually spent with her. She wore black ordinarily, had a marvelous dampness to her and trembled without control the first time they danced together. "Are you all right?" he kept asking. "Have you perhaps caught a chill?" There were some walks through town, one during which a truck backfired, causing Valurian to clutch at her arm as though it were a guardrail. "Oh, my God," she said, surprised, delighted and not at all to demean him, "I thought I was being protected." Her mother swooped down upon them one day, a great ship of a woman, catching Valurian in terrible clothes, needing a shave. In a restaurant, lit by ice-white fixtures, she spoke in an international accent and told them of her cattle investments and of killings at racetracks around the world; Valurian, still embarrassed about his shadowy face, prayed for the dinner to end. Later, he took them back to his rooming house and lit a fire; turning toward them, he saw that Carla had hopped into her mother's lap and gone to sleep in it like a little girl. He had never slept with her, although she gave him massive hints that it would be perfectly all right, indeed, highly preferred. "Oh, I'd love to be in a hotel somewhere," she would say as they danced. Or she would begin her trembling and say, rather hopelessly, "When I feel this way, whatever you do, don't take me out to some dark section of the woods." Ignoring the bait, he gave her aristocratic looks, as though he were an impeccable tennis star and she was insulting him by the inferior quality of her play. In truth, her dampness, the black skirts, the Indian squats, all were furnace-like and frightening to him. A boy named Harbinger had no such problems. She alerted him to Harbinger, saying she had run into the cutest fellow who lived in town and always hung his argyle socks out on the line where the girls could see them. It was as though she were giving him a last chance to get her into hotels or to sweep her out to cordoned-off sections of the woods. But he had always seen his affair with Carla—could he dignify it with that phrase?—as a losing battle, with perhaps a few brief successful forays before the final rout. One night, for example, he surprised her by batting out a few show tunes on the piano, singing along, too, through a megaphone, a talent he had kept up his sleeve. She almost tore his head off with her kisses, although, in retrospect, they were on the sisterly side. Toward the very end, he showed up on her dormitory steps with an alligator handbag, a Christmas gift she didn't quite know what to make of. Inevitably, she summoned him one day to talk over an ominous "little something"; polishing up his white buck shoes, he walked the length of the campus to her dormitory where she told him she had stayed out all night with the argyles boy and that she would not be seeing Valurian anymore. He called her a son of a bitch and for weeks afterward regretted being so clumsy and uncharming. There began for him a period of splendid agony. The first night, he was unable to eat and told a German exchange student—who had suffered many a rejection of his own—that any time he couldn't get fried chicken down he was really in trouble. A week later, he strolled by to see Carla as though nothing had happened; she told him that Harbinger was more in the picture than ever. She started off to rehearsals and he tailed her; she broke into a run, and he jogged right after her, as though it were perfectly normal to have conversations at the trot. On another occasion, he lay in wait for her outside the theater, grabbed her roughly and said, "Off to the woods we go. I have something to show you, something I'd been unwilling to show you before."

"What's that?" she asked, teasing him.

"You'll see," he said. But she wrenched herself away, an indication that Harbinger had already shown her plenty. He stayed away then for several months, taking up with a green-eyed Irish girl who had great torpedoing breasts, thought all Easterners were authentic gangsters and with no nonsense about it simply whisked *him* off to the woods. One night, before graduation, he went to a dance, feeling fine about being with the Irish girl, until Carla showed up with the argyles man. He continued to dance, but it was as though his entire back were frozen stiff. He saw her only one more time, paying her a good-bye visit and asking if he might have a picture. "No," she said. "I don't understand it," he said, "a lousy picture." But she held fast—and that was that.

He left school, went through the army as a second lieutenant in grain supply and then, for ten years or so, led a muted, unspectacular life, gathering in a living wage by doing many scattered fragments of jobs. He was fond of saying he "hit bottom" at age thirty, but, in truth, all that happened was that he developed asthma, got very frightened about it, saw a psychiatrist and, in the swiftest treatment on record, came upon a great springing trampoline of confidence that was to propel him, asthma and all, into seven years crowded with triumphs in the entertainment world—a part in a play that worked out well, a directing job that turned out even more attractively, films, more plays, television work and ultimately a great blizzard of activity that took a staff to keep track of.

From time to time, he had heard a little about her, not much—that she had gotten married quickly (not to the argyles man), had a child, gotten divorced. That she had settled in Delaware and never left. Although from time to time the thought of her flew into his mind, it was never a

and pray and let it go at that. The poor lost miserable wretch.

Oh well, he thought, screw her, and drove off for the big city.

—1970.

# Living Together

SHOT DOWN TWICE IN MARRIAGE, loser after a multitude of affairs, Pellegrino, in his forties, was about to pack it in romantically, when a fresh and delightful young woman suddenly bobbed up before him at a party like an apple in a barrel. Her eyes were wide, her movements graceful. She spoke with an ingratiating chuckle. Pellegrino's date was a good-natured blonde who had been raised in trailer courts and with whom he had come, characteristically, to a dead end. She could not have cared less—but the new woman was courteous and discreet, telling him only that she worked as an executive on the eighth floor of a well-known department store. When she wandered off to stand at the edge of the party, Pellegrino was far from smitten but full of questions. She wore a tweed jacket, tailored slacks, was somewhat older than the women he was used to. Was she too "responsible" for him? He had a charge card at her department store and enjoyed wandering through the men's clothing section. What if he simply showed up on the eighth floor? Would she dismiss him with a cynical laugh? He caught another glimpse of her and grappled with the most important question of all—did she have enough tush? A harsh, nonhumanistic concern for some, perhaps, but not for Pellegrino.

To be on the safe side, he made no effort to see her, shopping at a department store he wasn't that crazy about. Still, the idea of her nagged at him, that chuckle, the question of her body. Once in a while, he summoned her forth for a brief, slim-hipped fantasy in the night.

A year later, fate poked him in the ribs—he met her again at a reunion for people with strong Sixties concerns. He failed to recognize her; her hair was swept back, her great eyes tipsy over the rim of a cocktail glass. Was she a little faded around the edges? The hostess introduced them with great expectations. Pellegrino was correct, then swiftly went about his business—yet another blonde, a little overweight but at least a folk singer.

But she stubbornly kept after him—he remembered virtually swatting her away—until she yanked at his lapels and said, "Don't you even remember me? Katherine? The wedding reception?" The instant she identified herself, he realized he had been in love with her for a year, although he was, of course, careful not to tell her this. After a quick, forlorn look at the folk singer, he said he had thought about her a lot. What an amazing stroke of luck to run into her again. She said she had gone to Scotland to read books in solitude and had thought about him often, too. What a waste, they both agreed. He apologized for not recognizing her. But was it really his fault? "You've rearranged your hair," he said. Instantly, she reached back and let it fall, if not tumble—moving closer to the woman he remembered, though far from on the nose. He wanted to leave with her. Suddenly he realized that they had been talking across a wounded veteran in a wheelchair, her friend. He knew what that chuckle of hers was—compassion. To his everlasting shame, he made only reflexive small talk with the veteran, then yanked her away. In his defense, he could only tell himself 1) he was afraid of people in wheelchairs and 2) such was his love.

They tumbled through the streets to a restaurant he knew. Beneath the marquee she raised a horrified hand to her mouth and said, "Here!" Never in all the time he was to know her did she explain her resistance to the innocuous eating place. They took a table in the rear. For an hour or so he reveled in that sweet chuckle, his only possible disappointment in her being perhaps one reference too many to cartoons she had enjoyed in The New Yorker. As far as he knew, they were alone, bathed in a private light. Later, he found out the owner had observed them and told a cherished waiter: "Pellegrino is with a woman."

At midnight, on their way to an undecided destination, they kissed in the street, or rather, tried out each other's mouths with a happy result.

"It's probably not a good idea to go home together, is it?" she pleaded. Though he had arguments on hand to buttress both sides of the question, he more or less agreed.

"But half an hour after I see you again..." she trailed off. He tucked the promise away, as if in a wallet. They kissed again; this time he reached around through silk and was amazed he had ever questioned the excellence of her tush.

He could not honestly testify that he was counting the days until their next date, but when he saw her, he fell in love again, this time with her apartment, a floor-through in Murray Hill with sallow light and luxuriously worn furniture, the pieces confidently spaced apart—a serious person's home. (*Monastic* was the word that lingered.) Amazingly, they both owned copies of a bestselling poster. His was framed. In a masterstroke of carelessness, she had affixed hers to the wall with a thumbtack.

Breathlessly, she sparkled on. She came from a family of nurses. Twin brothers lived in China. Her favorite books? Ones written by retired members of the diplomatic corps. He sat in silence. From time to time, he glanced at his watch. Then he said: "Time's up."

"Oh my God, I didn't," she said.

"You did."

Dutifully, responsibly, she marched off to her loft bed, Pellegrino behind her, almost in step. The bed had no guardrail. One bad dream meant curtains for the sleeper. They made love, failing by some margin to enter paradise. But when he saw her dressing in the sallow light beneath

the staircase, his knees became weak; he flew at her sil-
houette.

And so they began to not quite live together. Three days
on, four days off. She raced to get him concert tickets,
artfully arranged his chair so that he was suddenly and
painlessly watching BBC productions. They slept together
at his place while her cats starved. Other nights, he packed
her off, clinging to his need to see strangers whom he no
longer enjoyed.

"Oh, please," she said to him one day, "let's live together."

"I'd do it," he said, "but I want it to come from me,
spontaneously." The next night it did. Finally, seamlessly,
after ten years of profitless fencing, Pellegrino shared his
life with another person. He waited for a heavy beam to
fall across his shoulders. Slowly, cautiously, he stood erect.

She took up perhaps a bit too much drawer space. But
she charmed his friends and cooked healthy, weightless
concoctions, making subtle use of garlic. Tirelessly she made
beds. She helped him with his work. Pellegrino, a writer
of movie trailers, was stuck one day, unable to break through
on a low-budget film—the theme, adolescent turmoil in
Eastern Europe. He mentioned it in bed. The next morning he found her huddled in a chair; she'd stayed up all
night, thinking he wanted her to come up with an entire
trailer on her own. He hugged her, told her that wasn't it
at all. Within minutes, she gave him a fresh angle of vision.
By tacit agreement, they called it encouragement, though
she did much more.

To a friend, he said, "She's made every moment of my
life a delight."

They traveled. He took her to his favorite hotels. She
approached them cautiously; then, to his slight irritation,
she seized them up as if they were her own discoveries.

To duck room service, they bought their own groceries. He sent her on ahead with bundles so that his entrance to the lobby could be formal. She made up songs with Pellegrino as the central character, spinning wild lyrics in the air; miraculously, when all seemed lost, she reined them in, got them to rhyme. She told him he was beautiful, that women took secret looks at him. "That's ridiculous," he said. But how could he help loving it when she said these things?

At night, with his nose pressed against the wool of her freshly laundered nightgown, he forgot for the moment about death.

But then things took a turn. The trailer business dried up, a casualty in a complex strike. At first Pellegrino felt unaffected, even amused. He had never been on strike before. Here was a chance to try out the sensation. He had planned to write a play on just such an occasion. He pounced on his typewriter. No play came. On a whim, they changed apartments, having been charmed by high ceilings and a rococo detail or two. They quickly saw it was a mistake— too long, too thin, a sliver of a space held out over raging midtown traffic as if by a hand. Pellegrino's daughter came to visit, fresh from art school, carrying prize-winning sketches and disapproval. Trying to please the child, she wound up serving undercooked hams. The three of them sat in silence at neighborhood restaurants, then returned to the small flat. Seeking privacy, they circled one another in cold geometric patterns. When the daughter left, Pellegrino pawed at the dirt while the strike took its grim toll.

To break up his afternoons, he took to watching foreign films at local art houses. One day, he gashed his wrist in the men's room of a culture complex. He thought of suing but lacked the energy. Holding a paper towel to the wound, he went upstairs to the movie house. There, while his blood pumped, he watched two hours of French irony.

He went back to the apartment to stare at his love. Oblivious to the screaming traffic, she sat beneath the louvered windows, sampling lightweight British mysteries. A tumbler of cognac, meant to be concealed, peeped out from behind a lamp base. She'd left her job to help Pellegrino, nursing him when he had no illness. Recently there had been talk of an advanced degree in international relations. It remained talk. She had taken on weight. He'd squinted his eyes to block out an extra chin. No longer could it be finessed. In the refrigerator, tins of gourmet macaroni came and went. Was it time to bring in the word *fat*?

He walked into the bedroom, actually a space created by a room divider, and wondered how he had reached this state, a serious fellow, age forty-five in view, with no booklined study. He looked at her side of the bed. When they first began to live together, she'd hollered out defiant antiwar cries in her sleep, left over from old Sixties rallies. He'd found this charming. Now she did great, silent, heaving rolls, an ocean liner during a stormy crossing. His choice was to lie on the floor or roll with her.

He walked back to the living room. She looked at him, as she always did, happy, expectant. In truth, she'd stayed away from stronger books for just such occasions; the mysteries could be interrupted at no great price. He told her he didn't have this in mind at all. The two of them crammed together in a skinny apartment. And he certainly hadn't known about the drinking. Did she think he wanted to team up with a juicer? (How he'd longed to use that word.) And it was high time they talked about the fat stuff. He wasn't talking about a few pounds, which he had to concede he had put on himself. He was talking full-out fat. Did the phrase El Grosserino mean anything to her? Was that part of their arrangement, that she would pork up for him? And what about the fabled women he was supposed to be allowed to see but somehow didn't? It's true, it's true, she'd said go right ahead, just don't fall in love. Well, that was some condition. They had talked about a child. Forget that, please. That's all he needed, a new family in a shitty apartment with a porked-up juicer.

She listened to all of this with a quizzical smile, as if somehow she had wandered into the wrong theater to see an odd play but was too generous or polite to leave. It was only when he said that he hated every single second of his life that the color ran out of her face. "All right then, go," she said. "Or *I'll* go." With lightning speed, as if sprung from a trap, she flashed across the room and lunged for a battered suitcase.

"No, no," he said, panicked, blocking her path, "never." With all his might, he hugged her to him, arms encircling her thick waist, which he was now convinced could be trimmed down after two or three weeks of intensive exercise.

"I wouldn't blow this for anything in the world."

—1981.

# Business
# is Business

**M**Y FATHER WORKED FOR A man named Schreever for twenty-five years. Schreever was the president of Schreever Laces, Inc. He was a boyhood friend of my father's and they started the business together. My father was not good at business manipulations. After a few years, he decided to devote himself exclusively to the factory and work on salary. It would be better that way since he would have fewer headaches. But as the business prospered, the factory expanded. My father had a dozen production assistants under him and about seventy-five women. He enjoyed being in charge of so many people. Even in his executive position, he was the first one down to the factory and the last one to leave in the evening. Everyone else on the street was certain my father owned half the business and he didn't really deny it. It was a flourishing business. But privately, to us, he said he had less headaches not having anything to do with the business end of it and he was tickled to death he didn't have to worry about those things. He invited me down to the factory once on a Saturday. I was in for the weekend from military school and it was a big thing for me because he'd never invited me down before.

The factory was deserted and my father switched on the lights. He took me around, showing me the piles of laces, rayons, silks, the sewing machines, patterns, and the cutting machines. "You really want to see something, kid?" he asked. He took a pile of rayon material in his hand and switched on the cutting machine. He slid the materials alongside the blade of the cutting machine and it sliced through the pile like a knife through soft butter. "What do you think of that?" he asked. I said it was pretty good. Actually, I didn't see what he was knocking himself out

about. If he hadn't been my father, and if this hadn't been
the first time he'd paid any attention to me I'd have told
him it was lousy and showed me nothing. My father went
inside to the latrine for a second. I wandered out of the
factory into the showroom where the finished laces were
on display for buyers. They were under glass and I went
up to the showcases and stared at them. My father ran up
behind me and slapped me across the mouth. I thought I
was too old to be slapped and for that reason I started to
cry as he tugged me back into the factory. "You don't ever
go where you're not supposed to go," he said. "I brought
you down here to see the factory. The showroom is someone else's territory," he said. Then he told me how many
girls he had under him, where they worked and how they
were always goofing off near the Coke machine and how
he had to be strict with them so they would learn not to
loaf. He told me how big the factory was, the exact di-
mensions. He told me the value of the factory in case
Schreever ever had to liquidate, which was highly improb-
able. A number of years later I saw a car lot attendant go
berserk in Cleveland. He leaped up on a Buick and beat
his chest telling the whole world that the sea of cars in the
lot belonged to him and no other man. The first thing I
thought of then was my father and his factory.

The first time I met Schreever was at my military school
graduation. I had always heard him mentioned in exalted
terms and I was scared when they brought him over to
me. Later, Cubby, a football player whom I idolized, told
me I was shaking like a leaf when I talked to him. I had
seen a picture of him with my father. They were at the
beach and they were both young. At that time it seemed
they were the same height. When I saw Schreever he was
actually much taller than my father. He asked me what I
was going to do later on. I told him I wanted to go to
college but I wasn't sure I knew what I wanted to take up.

"Going to college is a very expensive proposition," he told my father. "The boy ought to know exactly what he wants before he enters. I think he ought to consider something like accounting very seriously. Be a big help to him." My father agreed. He acted funny around Schreever, did a great deal of laughing. When Schreever asked where my mother was, my father hollered out "EDNA" across the parade grounds. My mother left three women and came running over. Schreever gave her a $25 defense bond for me.

When Schreever had his heart attack, I was living at home and going to school in the city. My mother had been after my father to ask for a share of the business and not go on all his life working for a salary. My father kept saying he didn't want the headaches. My mother said that Schreever had three homes and an apartment and we couldn't even have a place in the country every summer. My father said he'd see about it, but would she please leave it to him. "Besides," my father would say, "I'm sure Mrs. Schreever doesn't have an ermine stole like you do." That would always quiet my mother down and then my father would say he'd see about it anyway just to satisfy her although it would probably mean all kinds of headaches. Just at the time Schreever had the attack, two salesmen in the firm approached my father saying they were going to form their own outfit and would my father like to come along and be their "inside" man. He would be considered a full partner. My father was considering it when he went to see Schreever in the hospital. Schreever said it would all be over without my father. The business couldn't last a day without him and if he stayed on he could have a substantial raise in salary. Seeing Schreever dying in the hospital changed my father's mind. He turned down the two salesmen who decided not to go through with it without my father. Schreever got better and left the hospital.

My mother asked my father why he didn't ask for a share
in the business instead of settling for a raise. "You can't
do business with a dying man. You can't bargain with a
man who's had a heart attack. It's not ethical," my father
said. But this time he was plainly shaken. He seemed to
realize that he'd made a big, obvious mistake and he said
to my mother that when Schreever recuperated fully he
would "really talk to him this time."

Whether Schreever had made enough money and wanted
to take it easy the rest of his life or whether he'd been
given an ultimatum by the two salesmen was not plain. But
suddenly my father announced at dinnertime one night
that after twenty-five years in the lace business, Amos
Schreever was retiring. The new owners of Schreever Laces,
Inc. would be two of the firm's salesmen and himself. They
would all have to invest a considerable sum of money to
buy out Schreever. But the best part was yet to come. My
father had spoken to Schreever and out of gratitude for
twenty-five years of devoted service, Schreever was going
to put up my father's share of the investment.

Meanwhile, my father took his last cent out of the bank
as half of the investment and borrowed the other half from
my uncle, who was a gynecologist. Schreever would come
up with the money when it wasn't conspicuous so the other
partners, the two salesmen, would not be irritated and take
offense. "This is something that has to be kept very quiet,"
my father told us. "It's not good business ethics for
Schreever to be doing this for me. It's simply a gesture of
friendship and if the two salesmen found out it would be
horrible."

Still, an air of tension hung over our house as my father
started out in his new business venture. We had a dinner
during which we toasted his success, but everyone laughed
a little too easily and forced a good time. My mother was
told she would have to pull in on the household budget at

the beginning until things got straightened out. The lace business had its first bad season in twenty years. The buyers came in, took a great many numbers down, but really didn't buy too much. It was thought that Schreever had been a much stronger figure in the business than anyone realized and his absence was really hurting them. My mother, after a few months, asked my father at dinner if Schreever had been around recently and if Schreever had said anything to him. My father said Schreever was at his Florida home recuperating. "What's wrong with you, Edna?" he said. "A man in the condition he's in and you expect him to worry about business. You really don't understand anything." We got a letter from the Schreevers in Florida saying the weather was wonderful and then another from them in New Orleans. My father laughed nervously and said it was good they were getting around. He hoped it was doing the old boy's health some good.

Living at home, the way I was, it was easy for me to see the change that had come over my father. He was obviously upset constantly, but it came out in a very strange way. He began to bring his factory home with him. Everything in the house had to be done in a precise, exacting way. He went around piling and lining things up. At the dinner table, he would scrape the crumbs off the tablecloth with a knife after dinner, getting every·single one even if it took half an hour. Once I took some butter from a side of the dish that hadn't been started and he knocked the knife out of my hand. He went around cleaning and dusting and making things neat. He made his bed over at night in distinct motions as if he were doing it by the numbers. He grew further apart from my mother. She asked him whether Schreever had gotten in touch with him, and he said, "Shut your goddamned mouth." Another time she asked him in another way and he said, "You know it *is* possible I mis-understand him. That's been known to happen in the history of men, too. Maybe I took something for granted that really wasn't the case." But it didn't sound as though he meant it. As business got worse, we continued to hope that Schreever would come through.

When my father had an attack of sciatica and had to sleep on a board, we took a place in the country near a lake. The rental was pretty high and my sister and nephew came to live with us. There was the talk, of course, that my father's illness was mainly psychological, but at any rate, it was painful. He was stationed in the parlor and we had to tiptoe past him. The slightest creak would start him groaning. We tried to make everything pleasant for him and keep his mind off business, but he was on the phone every day speaking to his place.

I lied about my age and took a job as a policeman across the lake. I was to carry a gun and keep unauthorized people off the private beach. The gun scared me out of my wits. But at night I would swim the lake to our side. That always refreshed me and I would not think about the gun until the next day. I always had the feeling it would go off in the holster and take my leg off.

One night I swam the lake and came home. I changed my clothes and went into the back room for a game of GRIPs with my nephew, Harry, who was five years old. We made up the game and it used to drive him crazy. I would get him in a grip, making up a name for it, saying it was an Elementary Alligator Grab or an Advanced Boa hold, and no man had ever gotten out of it. He would start to laugh and then I would get him in the grip and after a while ease up, letting him slip out. When he got out he would squeal with delight, begging me to get him in an Intermediate Japanese Panther Lock. I had him in one of the grips when my mother came over to the side of my father's board and said she had a card from the Schreevers. My father didn't say anything. She said she would read it.

It was from Naples and it said, "Dear Henry and Edna, Are enjoying sunny Italy and will go on from here to Switzerland. Europe is truly wonderful, everything we ever dreamed of. Will see England if there is time and we don't get too overtired. Hope you and family are enjoying best of health, we remain, the Schreevers." My mother showed my father the card which showed the Schreevers standing in front of some ruins. I saw it later and Mr. Schreever looked tall and suntanned, better than at my graduation. My father turned away and said, "You're always digging me, Edna. All my life you've been digging me. And now that I'm sick you're digging me worse than ever."

We drove home in a gloom at summer's end, stopping every couple of miles because the radiator got overheated. My father had his tonsils taken out, which seemed to cure his back ailment. There was no talk of Schreever or business on the way home or in the house for the next month. We were certain it was all over and my father *had* really misunderstood him.

One Monday night, after working overtime, my father flung open the door, whisked my mother off her feet and blurted out, "The Schreevers are back. They called me at work. They want us to come up to their Connecticut place on Sunday."

My mother was more excited than she'd been in a long time. She made him calm down and tell the story slowly at the dinner table. Mr. Schreever, it seems, had called my father while he was in the factory, telling him he was having a little cocktail party on Sunday and would he like to come and bring along the wife and boy. There would be no one else there and they could have a nice little talk during the afternoon.

We had a victory drink and my father chided my mother for being so silly all these last months. "You don't understand business ethics, Edna," he said. "Number one, the man was a sick man, and number two, it just would've been lousy if he'd done something for me and those partners of mine found out about it."

My mother spent the rest of the week selecting a new outfit. A new suit was bought for me. The car was Simonized and my father had his nails manicured. He took a sunlamp treatment at the barbershop and came back with a fairly good tan. My mother had her stole cleaned and brushed and her hair done at the beauty parlor. Just before we started out, my mother suggested that maybe we oughtn't take the car. "After all, they're smart people. When they see a convertible they may think we're doing very well. You never know, Henry, they might think we have property investments."

"That just shows you how much you know about business," my father said. "Get in, Edna, and stop your nonsense. If you've been in business just two days you know that it's always best to look your very nicest. No one wants to have anything to do with a slob."

We drove up with the top down and the air nice and cool. My father got some good music on the radio. A sign on one of the turnoffs said Sunny Roads Estate—The Schreevers—and we turned in. The driveway seemed about a mile long. There were many little houses along the way to the main house. In front of it stood the Schreevers, both dressed very simply but graciously. Mrs. Schreever had a boxer heeling at her side. They greeted us and the first thing they commented on was the car and how well we all looked. "A con—*ver*—tible," Mrs. Schreever said. "Isn't it beautiful. And look how wonderful she looks. And that suntan on Henry. And look at that lovely stole on Edna. My, you look *won-der-ful,* my dears."

I was given the boxer to play with and my parents went into the bar to drink. They talked for about an hour, all about the Schreevers' European trip and how they had found all sorts of perfumes and gifts over there to take back. Then Schreever brought up the old days and how they had both started out together and how far they had come over the years. Everyone got a little tipsy except my mother. My father did a great deal of laughing and smiling whenever Schreever opened his mouth. The hours went by. My mother started to poke my father. He looked at her like she was insane. She kept poking him, casually so no one would see, but he kept smiling and laughing at Mr. Schreever. They talked about Abel Starr, a boyhood friend of theirs who had gone to prison and how they had both visited him; they kidded about how they had discussed slipping a file to him in a cake. It got dark on the porch and then we were up and saying good-bye, my mother still prodding my father, and my father still smiling and laughing with Mr. Schreever. Then we were in the car driving home, my father a little tipsy and my mother silent. After a while, he seemed to realize what had happened. My mother didn't say a word. "I guess it was just meant to be a little social gathering after all, Edna. It's really not good business to talk about money at someone's house. It'd be a sorry mess if I was to go and ask for money when someone had invited me over for cocktails." My mother asked him to stop the car. He pulled over and she threw up at the side of the road. She came back crying in a loud, snuffling way. My father put his arm around her as he drove, saying he really would ask him in the city. No more fooling around. All of us knew that moment that he would never ask him. It was the first time I had ever seen my mother cry. But it was also the first time I had ever seen my father put his arm around her.

—1956.

# The Mourner

ONE DAY, MARTIN GANS FOUND himself driving out to the Long Island funeral of Norbert Mandel, a total stranger. A habit of his was to take a quick check of the obit section in the New York *Times* each day, concentrating on the important deaths, then scanning the medium-famous ones and some of the also-rans. The listing that caught his eye on this particular day was that of Norbert Mandel, although Gans did not have the faintest idea why he should be interested in the passing of this obscure fellow. The item said that Mandel, of Syosset, Long Island, had died of a heart attack at the age of seventy-three, leaving behind two sisters, Rose and Sylvia, also one son, a Brooklyn optometrist named Phillip. It said, additionally, that Mandel had served on an East Coast real-estate board and many years back had been in the Coast Guard. An ordinary life, God knows, with nothing flashy about it, at least on the surface. Gans read the item in a vacant, mindless way, but suddenly found his interest stirred, a fire breaking out with no apparent source. Was it the sheer innocuousness of the item? Of Mandel's life? He traveled on to other sections of the paper, sports and even maritime, but the Mandel story now began to prick at him in a way that he could not ignore; he turned back to the modest paragraph and read it again and again, until he knew it by heart and felt a sweeping compulsion to race out to Mandel's funeral, which was being held in a memorial chapel on the south shore of Long Island.

If this had happened at some idle point in his life, it might have made some sense. But Gans was busier than ever, involved in moving his ceramics plant to a new location on Lower Fifth Avenue, after twenty years of being in the same place. It was aggravating work; even after the

153

move, it would take six months before Gans really settled
in to the new quarters. Yet you could hardly call Mandel's
funeral a diversion. A trip to Puerto Rico would have been
that. Nor was Gans the type of fellow who particularly
enjoyed funerals. His mother and father were still living.
No one terribly close to him had died up to now, just some
aunts and uncles and a couple of nice friends whose deaths
annoyed rather than grieved him. Gans had probably con-
tributed to one aunt's death, come to think of it. A woman
in the hospital bed next to Aunt Edna had attacked a book
the visiting Gans held under his arm. Gans struck back,
defending the volume, and a debate began over poor Aunt
Edna's head, as she fought a tattered intravenous battle
for life.

The day of Mandel's funeral, Gans took a slow drive to
the memorial chapel, allowing an extra half hour for possible traffic problems and the chance that he might lose
his way on the south shore, which had always been tricky
going for him. On the way, he thought a little about Mandel. He pictured him in an overcoat, also with a beard,
although a totally nonrakish one. Mandel struck him as
being a tea drinker and someone who dressed carefully
against the cold, owning a good stock of mufflers and
galoshes. Gans did not particularly like Mandel's associa-
tion with the East Coast real-estate board, but at the same
time, he saw him as a small property owner, not really that
much at home with the big boys and actually a decent fellow
who was a soft touch. He liked the sound of Mandel's two
sisters, Rose and Sylvia, envisioning them as buxom, good-
natured, wonderful cooks, enjoying a good pinch on the
ass, provided it remained on the hearty and nonerotic side.
Phillip, the optometrist, struck Gans as being a momma's
boy, into a bit of a ball-breaking marriage, but not too bad
a fellow; the Army, Gans felt, had probably toughened
him up a bit. There was a chance, of course, that Gans was

completely wide of the mark, but these were his specula-
tions as he breezed out to the chapel to get in on the funeral
of Norbert Mandel, a fellow he didn't know from Adam.

The chapel was part of an emporium that lay just outside
a shopping center and was used as well for bar mitzvahs
and catered affairs of all kinds. An attendant in a chauf-
feur's uniform took his car, saying, "No sweat, I'll see it
don't get wet." Inside the carpeted chapel, a funeral-parlor
employee asked him if he were there, perchance, for Ben-
jamin Siegal. "No, Norbert Mandel," said Gans. The attendant said they had Mandel on the second floor. Before
climbing the stairs, Gans stopped to relieve himself in the
chapel john and realized he always did that before going
in to watch funeral services. Did this have some significance, he wondered, a quick expulsion of guilt, a swift
return to a pure state? Or was it just the long drives?

There was only a small turnout for Mandel. Those on
hand had not even bothered to spread out and make the
place seem a little busier. Mandel's friends and relatives
were all gathered together in the first half dozen rows,
giving the chapel the look of an off-Broadway show that
had opened to generally poor notices. Gans estimated that
he was about fifteen minutes early, but he had the feeling
that few additional mourners were going to turn up and
he was right about that. Somehow he had sensed that Mandel was not going to draw much of a crowd. Was that why
he had come? To help the box office? Come to think of
it, funeral attendance had been on his mind for some time.
He had been particularly worried, for example, that his
father, once the old man went under, would draw only a
meager crowd. His father kept to himself, had only a sprin-
kling of friends. If Gans had to make up a list of mourners
for his dad, he was sure he would not be able to go beyond
a dozen the old man could count on to turn up, rain or
shine. This was troubling to Gans: in addition, he won-

dered what there was a rabbi could actually say about his dad. That he was a nice man, kept his nose clean? First of all, he wasn't that nice. People see an old grandmother crossing a street and assume she's a saint. She might have been a triple ax murderer as a young girl in Poland and gotten away with it, thanks to lax Polish law enforcement. Who said old was automatically good and kind? Who said old and short meant gentle and well meaning? Gans' own funeral was an entirely different story. He wasn't worried much about that one. At least not about the turnout. He had a million friends and they would be sure to pack the place. His mother, too, could be counted on to fill at least three quarters of any house: if you got a good rabbi, who knew something about her, who could really get her essence, there wouldn't be much of a problem in coming up with send-off anecdotes. She didn't belong to any organizations, but she had handed out plenty of laughs in her time. It would be a tremendous shame if she were handled by some rabbi who didn't know the first thing about her. He had often thought of doing his mother's eulogy himself; but wouldn't that be like a playwright composing his own notices?

Gans felt a little conspicuous, sitting in the back by himself, and didn't relax until three middle-aged ladies came in and took seats a row in front of him. He had them figured for cousins from out of town who had taken a train in from Philadelphia. They did not seem deeply pained by the loss of Mandel and might have been preparing to see a Wednesday matinee on Broadway. Their combined mood seemed to range from aloof to bitter, and Gans guessed they were on the outs with the family, probably over some long-standing quarrel involving the disposition of family jewelry and china. Gans had little difficulty picking out Rose and Sylvia, Norbert's sisters, who were seated in the front row, wearing black veils and black fur coats.

They wept and blew their noses and seemed deeply troubled by Mandel's death, which had come out of the blue. Phillip, the only son, was a complete surprise to Gans. Gans assumed he was the one who was wedged between Rose and Sylvia in the front row. He was certainly no momma's boy. He was every bit of six-three and you could see beneath his clothes that he was a bodybuilder. His jaw was tight, his features absolutely perfect, and you simply wouldn't want to mess with him. Let a woman get smart with this optometrist and she'd wind up with her head in the next county. What woman would want to get smart with him? Jump through a few hoops is what a girl would prefer doing for this customer.

The rabbi came out at a little trot, a slender fellow with brown disappearing hair and rimless glasses—ideal, Gans felt, for a career in crime investigation, since he was totally inconspicuous. Gans did not know much about rabbis, but when this fellow began to speak, he could see that his was the "new style"; that is, totally unflamboyant, low-pressure, very modest, very Nixon Administration in his approach to the pulpit. As he spoke, one of the sisters, either Rose or Sylvia, cried in the background, the bursts of tears and pity coming at random, not really coinciding with any particularly poignant sections in the rabbi's address. "I regret to say that I did not know the departed one very well," he began. "However, those close to him assure me that this was, indeed, my great loss. The late Norbert Mandel, whom we are here to send to his well-earned rest this day, was, by all accounts, a decent, fair, kind, generous, charitable man who led a totally exemplary life." He went on to say that death, sorrowful as it must seem to those left behind in the valley of the living, was not a tragedy when one looked upon it as a life-filled baton being passed from one generation to another or, perhaps, as the satisfying final act of a lifetime drama, fully and truly lived. "And who

can say this was not the case with the beloved Norbert
Mandel, from his early service to his country in the Coast
Guard, right along to his unstinting labors on behalf of
the East Coast real-estate board; a life in which the unsel-
fish social gesture was always a natural reflex, rather than
something that had to be painfully extracted from him."

"Hold it right there," said Gans, rising to his feet in the
rear of the chapel.

"Shame," said one of the Philadelphia women.

"What's up?" asked the rabbi.

"You didn't even know this man," said Gans.

"I recall making that point quite early in my remarks,"
said the rabbi.

"How can you just toss him into the ground?" said Gans.
"You haven't told anything about him. That was a man
there. He cut himself a lot shaving. He had pains in his
stomach. Why don't you try to tell them how he felt when
he lost a job? The hollowness of it. Why don't you go into
things like his feelings when someone said kike to him the
first time? What about all the time he clocked worrying
about cancer? And then didn't even die from it. How did
he feel when he had the kid, the boy who's sitting over
there? What about the curious mixture of feelings toward
his sisters, the tenderness on one hand and, on the other
hand, the feelings he couldn't exercise, because you're not
allowed to in this society? How about some of that stuff,
rabbi?"

"And they're just letting him talk," said one of the Philadelphia women.

"They're not throwing him out," said another. But Rose
and Sylvia kept sobbing bitterly, so awash in sorrow the
sisters appeared not to have even realized that Gans had
taken over from the rabbi. Gans was concerned about only
one person, the well-built son Phillip; but, to his surprise,
the handsome optometrist only buried his head in his hands,

as though he were a ballplayer being scolded at half time by an angry coach. The rabbi was silent, concerned, as though the new style was determined to be moderate and conciliatory, no matter what went on in the chapel. It's a big religion, the rabbi seemed to be saying by his thoughtful silence, with plenty of room for the excessive.

Up until now, it had been a kind of exercise for Gans, but the heat of his own words began to excite him. "Can you really say you're doing justice to this man?" he asked. "Or are you insulting him? Do you know how he felt? Do you know anything about his disappointments? How he wanted to be taller? To you, he's Norbert Mandel, who led an exemplary life. What about the women he longed for and couldn't get? How he spent half his life sunk in grief over things like that. And the other half picking his nose and worrying about getting caught at it. Do you know the way he felt about yellow-haired girls and how he went deaf, dumb and blind when one he liked came near him? Shouldn't some of that be brought out? He wanted blondes right into his seventies; but did he ever get a taste of them? Not on your life. It was Mediterranean types all the way. Shouldn't you take a minute of your time to get into how he felt about his son, the pride when the kid filled out around the shoulders and became tougher than Norbie would ever be, and the jealousy, too, that made him so ashamed and guilty? Do you have any idea what he went through, playing the kid a game, beating him and then wanting to cut off his arm for it? Then letting the kid win a game and that was no good, either. You act as though you've scratched the surface. Don't make me laugh, will you please. You know about his vomiting when he drank too much? On the highway. How do you think that felt? What about a little something else you're leaving out? Those last moments when he knew something was up and he had to look death right in the face. What was that for him, a picnic? I'll tell you, rabbi, you ought to pull him right out of the coffin and take a look at him and find out a little bit about who you're talking about."

"There was a time," said Phillip, the sole surviving son, as though he had received a cue, "when he left the family for a month or so. He was around, but he wasn't with us. He got very gray and solemn and didn't eat. We found out it was because an insurance doctor told him he had a terrible heart and couldn't have life insurance. He called him an 'uninsurable.' That was something, having an uninsurable for a dad. It was a mistake—his heart was healthy at the time—but it was the longest month of my life. The other time that comes to mind is when he shut someone up on the el when we were going out to Coney Island. Shut him up like you never saw anyone shut up. Guy twice his size."

"Very touching," said the rabbi. "Now may I ask how you knew the deceased?"

"I used to see him around," said Gans.

"Fine," said the rabbi. "Well, I don't see why we can't have this once in a while. And all be a little richer for it. If the family doesn't object. Do you have anything else?"

"Nothing I can think of," said Gans. "Unless some of the other members of the family would like to sound off a bit."

"He had a heart of solid gold," said one of the sisters.

"He was some man," said the other.

"Sounds like he was quite a fellow," said the rabbi.

Gans had no plan to do so originally but decided now to go out to the burial grounds, using his own car instead of accepting the offered ride in one of the rented limousines. After Mandel had been put into the ground, Gans accepted an offer from one of the sisters, whom he now knew to be Rose, to come back and eat with the family in a Queens delicatessen. Gans' own mother had always been contemptuous of that particular ritual, mocking families who were able to wolf down delicatessen sandwiches half an hour after a supposedly beloved uncle or cousin had been tossed into the earth. "They're very grief-stricken," she would say, "you can tell by their appetites." Gans, as a result, had developed a slight prejudice against the custom, although the logical part of him said why not eat if you're hungry and not eat if you're not. There seemed to be a larger crowd at the delicatessen than had been at the funeral. And it wasn't delicatessen food they were eating, either; it was Rose's cooking. Evidently, the family had merely taken over the restaurant for the afternoon, but Rose had brought in her own food. Gans had some difficulty meeting young Phillip's eyes and Phillip seemed equally ill at ease with him. Gans could not get over how wrong he had been about the boy. He had had an entirely different feeling about what a Brooklyn optometrist should look like. This fellow was central casting for the dark-haired hero in Hollywood Westerns. Even the right gait, slow and sensual; Gans wondered if he had ever thought seriously about a career in show business. Gans ate a hearty meal, and there was something in his attack on the food that seemed to indicate he had earned it. He sat at the same table as Phillip, who ate dreamily, speculatively and seemed, gradually, to get comfortable with the mysterious visitor who had taken over the funeral service.

"You know," said Phillip, "a lot of people never realized this, but he was one hell of an athlete. He had two trophies for handball, and if you know the Brooklyn playground league, you know they don't fool around. And a guy once offered him a tryout with the Boston Bees." The boy paused then, as if he expected a nostalgic anecdote in return from Gans.

Instead, Gans took a deep breath, tilted his chair back

slightly and said, "I have to come clean, I never met the man in my life."

"What do you mean?" said Phillip, hunching his big shoulders a bit, although he seemed more puzzled than annoyed. "I don't understand."

Gans hesitated a moment, looking around at the sisters, Rose and Sylvia, at the cousins from Philly, who seemed much more convivial, now that they were eating, at the rabbi, who had come over for a little snack, and at the other mourners. He complimented himself on how easily he had fitted into the group, and it occurred to him that most families, give or take a cousin or two, are remarkably similar, the various members more or less interchangeable.

"I don't know," he said, finally, to the blindingly handsome optometrist, sole surviving offspring of the freshly buried Norbert Mandel. "I read about your dad in the paper and I had the feeling they were just going to throw him into the ground, and that would be the end of him. Bam, kaput, just like he never lived. So I showed up."

"Now that I think of it," he said, reaching for a slice of Rose's *mohn* cake and anticipating the crunch of poppy seeds in his mouth, "I guess I just didn't think enough of a fuss was being made."

—1970.

# The Pledges

**E**ASED OUT OF A JOB, Gonder went around pleading poverty, but secretly had six months taken care of; he felt anxious nonetheless and from those close to him sought pledges of love. For six years running, Gonder's mother had alternated Sunday visits, one to his sister in Philly, one to Gonder's house, in the shadow of the Throgs Neck Bridge. One day, standing on an unemployment line, he suddenly flew into a phone booth and called his mother, begging her to cancel out those visits to Philly.

"Of course I'll do it," she said, "but why the sudden love?"

"I can't explain it," he said. "It's just till I get on my feet."

"What'll I tell Francy?"

"Stall her," he said. "Tell her you'll write."

With only an occasional interview in the picture, Gonder had plenty of time on his hands. In this situation, most men laid low. Gonder went the other way, seeing to it he had plenty of company. Thursday nights were for dinner with Vandallo, his one Negro friend, a higher-up in the fight for housing. After one of the meals, Gonder invited the fair-housing official up to his study. They tossed down brandies and Gonder asked, straight out, if the man was really his friend. In the past few weeks, he'd often found himself throwing out that question.

"Pretty good friends," said Vandallo, "although I got to admit the gap between the races is widening these days."

Gonder then went into the closet and hauled out an old straitjacket; years back, an uncle named Harlan had been committed to an institution, then released. He had asked for and mysteriously gotten to keep the jacket. Gonder, a child then, had played with it at his cured uncle's house, turned it into a toy and wound up hanging onto it.

165

"It's awfully important to me," Gonder said to his friend. "I'd like you to slip into this."

"Not for no man, baby."

"It's a little piece of a dream," said Gonder. "The only part I remember. Anyway, I really would appreciate it. You said you were my friend."

"I'll get in there all right," said Vandallo, rising from his chair. "When I'm dead about six times over." Minutes later, he scooped up his wife and left Gonder's house as though he were storming out of a housing rhubarb.

Shaky over the turndown, Gonder walked back and forth along his bookshelves, flicking the bindings of novels with one finger, his kind of pacing. At four in the morning, the doorbell rang. Vandallo.

"I figure I'm setting back the whole movement this way," he said, pushing his way in. "Anyway, how long I got to stay in that thing?"

"A couple of minutes," said Gonder, leading him upstairs. "It's just the idea of it."

"I think it's some kind of a symbol to me," he said, lacing up his friend. "Maybe I should see a shrink."

"Save the bread," said Vandallo, his arms immobilized. "What you tryin' to do is stifle the brothers."

Gonder referred to his friend Brecker as a "drinking buddy," although they rarely drank. With no cause for stealth, he would tell his wife he was going for a drive, then steal out late at night and meet Brecker at a cabaret. Some called Brecker Gonder's protégé. Others said Gonder had the slim, homely, public-relations man in his pocket. Gonder himself felt a certain mastery over his friend, although he had never exploited this feeling. There was nothing to exploit. Their conversation was light and fluffy. "You're a guy I can talk to," Brecker would say and at least once an evening he would make the confession that Gon-

der was "better company than a broad." For years the
unmarried Brecker had eked out a slim existence. More
recently he had turned up with a fairly good job, one that
got him trips to Arab countries and, on occasion, neat
bonuses. One night Gonder slipped out to meet his friend,
just in from Kuwait. He listened to desert anecdotes for a
while and then, with a hand on Brecker's shoulder, broke
in on one and said: "Hey, look, you're always saying we
can talk pretty well, right? We don't hold things back."

"Sometimes I worry about that," said Brecker. "Why I
can't have that with a girl."

"All right, then *this* is what I'm not holding back. Look,
I can't stand your having a job and me not. That's what it
boils down to. I don't know whether it's a competitive thing,
what. It isn't even something unconscious. It's right out
there and it's giving me fits. I'll only ask you this once, but
I got to ask you to unload it. You know, quit."

"What are you, crazy?" said Brecker, getting to his feet
in his greatest show of independence. "What do you think,
I can just get these anytime I want them?"

"I say you can," said Gonder. "You're getting better and
better in your field. Look, if it was really a great job, I'd
chalk myself off as sick in the head and I'd never even
make a suggestion like this. But the job's no bargain.

"In the long run, pulling out has got to help you."

Brecker held out two weeks, then phoned Gonder in the
middle of the night.

"I told the bastards to shove it today," he said. "Anyway,
I couldn't take all the traveling."

"You made the right move," said Gonder.

"Listen," said Brecker, "I'm a little shaky. Can you take
a run down to Vinnie's and meet me for a while?"

"I can't handle it now," said Gonder, free as a bird. "I'll
call you when I'm clear."

After a tempestuous first marriage, Gonder had gone sailing into another. His goal: Plenty of calm. His new wife, a little older, less pretty, had served it up in great quantities. They had peaceful days, peaceful dinners, quiet nights. After four months of being out on the streets, Gonder typed up a document: "I, Cissie Gonder, testify that for the rest of my days I will remain faithful to my husband, and have no affairs whatsoever." One night, after a calm, bordering-on-the-lethargic dinner, meatless to conserve money, Gonder spread out the document and said, "Hey, honey, read this, just for fun." Without picking up the paper, she scanned it quickly and said, "Okay, I read it, what's the deal?"

"You wouldn't consider signing something like that, would you?"

"No, I wouldn't," she said and with great patience began to stack the dishes.

She was no lead-pipe cinch. He kept at her and after half a dozen tries, some casual, others insistent, he forced her to flick off the TV one night and say, "Look, I've really had my bellyful. I don't even want to see that thing again, don't want to discuss it. No, I don't have any ideas or anything, but I wouldn't sign that paper if my life depended on it." She'd kept her calm, but there was a dangerous first-marriage note in her voice and Gonder retreated.

Actually, she had given him little cause for concern. There had been a Syrian doorman at their first apartment building who might have turned into a problem, but the budding affair—if Gonder wanted to dignify it by that title—had gone up in smoke when they bought a house. She made no bones about still feeling an "attraction" for her first husband, but he had gone to Rome to make films and they had gotten a card saying he was probably going to settle in and give up his citizenship. One day Gonder tore up the document and threw it out of a bus window; but that night he typed up another.

He caught her finally, drugged, half asleep. The one lamp gave the bedroom a cold Roman look. "Please, honey," he said, slipping it under her nose with a pen. "Oh, shit," she said, scrawling her name and then turning over with a great thump. "Thanks, babe," he said, kissing her hair and flicking off the light. Unable to sleep, he tiptoed up to his study, kicked his legs up on a desk. Vandallo was in his pocket. His mother came regularly on Sundays. Brecker had been out of work for a month. He unfurled the document and triumphantly read his second wife's pledge of fidelity. Beaming, he lit up a cigar. Now he felt better. Now he was all set.

—1967.

# A Different Ball Game

**B**ILLY RIEGELSON STOPPED TALKING TO his mother the night he told her he wasn't going to take the trip to the Orient she had promised him and was going to marry a Trailways hostess instead. She was drunk when he delivered the news; to soften the blow, he gave her a present for a birthday she'd had the week before and, without opening it, she skimmed it right at his face and probably would have blinded him in one eye if she had hit him. The present was a Spanish mantilla he had bought at Saks and for all he knew she never found this out. He was hurt, and the rush of his tears was genuine, but he was probably not as wounded as he made out to be. He tightened up his fists, shut his eyes and hissed out the words: "Oh, boy, a birthday present...a *birthday* present...and that's what you did with it...."

After a hopeless little shrugging movement, he walked out of her apartment and did not speak to her for eight or nine years, he wasn't sure. For all he knew, his mother might have spent the entire period thinking if she hadn't flung the present she still would have had a devoted son. She was probably much smarter than that. As for Billy Riegelson, he, of course, knew better. He was simply sick of her and was looking for an opening, some foolproof incident, so that he could make his move. He had had twenty-six years of hearing how great her figure was, how every man in every room everywhere was crazy about her, how nobody could give and receive love the way she could, and how tragic it was that she had to sit in the background while Billy Riegelson's dad went to work because, after all, she was the one with the "business head." He had had a bellyful.

And then the drinking topped it off. She was no prize

package before the drinking got out of hand, but there had always been a certain charm to her excesses. It went up in smoke when she started to polish off a quart a day. People in the family, including Billy Riegelson's dad, were afraid to say she had a little problem there. Small wonder. Standing on the living-room carpet at midnight, swaying back and forth in her nightgown and with a full load on, she made quite a monumental and frightening spectacle. "Your mother's turning out to be quite a problem," Leonard Riegelson would complain to his son. "Boy, have I got my hands full." But to listen to him you would never know he had a full-scale alcoholic on his hands. Billy Riegelson was the only one in the family with the nerve to call his mother a lush and he felt like quite a hero each time he said, "Can't you see she's a boozehound," or "For Christ's sake, dad, my mother's a drunk." Banging out the words "lush" and "boozehound" gave him particular pleasure. But, of course, he never said any of these words directly to his mother either.

And then he simply dropped out of the picture and let his dad and three sisters wrestle with her. He heard she had had to be sent to a hospital to dry out and get a psychiatric check; how he managed to stay out of that one was a mystery to him. He was a little afraid of his Trailways wife and somehow he must have figured that by freezing out his mother he was piling up points with her, showing his wife he was an independent fellow. When he learned that his mother had to go to the hospital a second time, he made plans to visit her, but she got out fast and then a sister told him she had gotten a good scare and had really given up the sauce this time. "The sauce" was his expression. He kept his distance. He had gotten in early on the making of TV commercials, the dazzling, quick-sputtering ones that had begun to influence feature films and were considered to be an art form in some circles. In truth, the one thing he missed from his mother was her ability to make a fuss over him and over his work. She just didn't give a damn who was around and who might be listening. Whenever he showed her something of his, a photograph, a poem, a shirt he had bought, anything, she would clutch at her throat and say, "Wait a minute, I can't breathe. Hold on a second....Well, it's insane, absolutely insane... crazy....I've never seen anything like it in my life." She would react to the work with her whole body as though it were giving her a fit right out on the street. It was a style that was the total opposite of cool. He didn't care that it was overdone, embarrassing; he simply loved the shows she put on for him and there was no one in the world who could top her when it came to eating up his achievements.

Things changed. After nine years of being married, Billy Riegelson's wife decided she really wasn't ready to settle down and was going to Iran to work things out. He couldn't figure out why she had to go that far, but then he heard about an Iranian army pilot who was going to the Far East with her so that she wouldn't have to work things out all by herself. Riegelson also learned that the pilot was a terrific dancer. There were some grim and bumpy nights when he certainly would have enjoyed talking to his mother, but he held off and wondered, come to think of it, why she didn't call him. He waited for his personal life to clarify. It had a way of not clarifying. His wife returned from Iran but immediately started making advance preparations to go back the following summer. She was going to spend her summers in Iran. It was the way she had come up with of working things out. She said there was no point in trying to talk her out of it. When she was forty-six or so she might be ready to settle down. Billy Riegelson hooked up with a young, quiet actress who had a terrific voice and came up with one great remark every now and then, usually around the time she sensed he was going to drop her. Once, after an argument, she started to cry and said, "The day I met you I should have stocked up on waterproof mascara." The remarks, come to think of it, were not that great, but they were far above the level of her standard material, and they always made him wonder if he weren't letting something good get away. So he hung on to her.

One day he called his mother. "How are you doing, kid," he said.

"You still call your mother 'kid'?" she said.

He laughed and she said, "I heard the chuckle. My boy's chuckle. When I hear that I know everything's all right. And I can sleep." He made a lunch date with "the kid" and what a change in her! She looked much older, but the aging had an attractive color to it and he could not help feeling it was the first time in his life she had ever really come across to him as a mother and not a faded Ziegfeld girl. She had stopped dyeing her hair yellow and let it go to a natural gray. It had a soft, finespun look to it. She had put on some weight, but hadn't bothered to knock herself out about it and press it down with foundation garments. She had just let it exist and it seemed fine. Her face was deeply seamed, not just with a hint of aging, but with the serious markings of old age now, and that threw him a bit and also melted any of his resistance to her. She put on a modest version of one of her old productions with the waiter, calling him "Sweetheart" and "Doll" and asking him how in the world an attractive-looking fellow like him had wound up as a waiter. When the fellow asked if she would like a drink, she said, "No you don't, baby, I know what you're trying to get me to do." But the bald, uncomfortable, attacking sexuality was gone; her style now was just a bit flirtatious, but mostly gentle, vulnerable, of all things, shy, a word he thought he would never live to see himself apply to his old lady. All the iron had dropped out of her.

She needled him a few times about all the time that had passed since they last spoke. He referred to it as an eight-year period and she corrected him: "As long as we're being mathematical," she said, "it's nine." He laid the blame for the long silence on some of the troubles he had been having with his wife, and his mother said not to worry, she knew all about it and really felt for him. A few times she reverted to her old style. "What's that fellow eating?" she asked the waiter, referring to a chap in the corner. "It certainly looks delicious."

"It only looks good because it's on another table," said Riegelson. He told her he was amazed she was still doing that, involving herself in other people at other tables and assuming they were more interesting than whomever she was sitting with. She promised not to do it again.

Toward the end of the meal, she looked up shyly and said, "Do I get a little kiss?"

"What for?" he asked.

"I haven't had a drink in fifteen months."

He thought her way of presenting the news was most appealing and he did give her a little kiss. He also made another lunch date with her, for the following week. He began to have lunch with her once a week; then, without any fanfare, he upped the meetings to two a week, picking giant, quiet restaurants and going in around two in the afternoon when regular jobholders began to go back to work and you could really settle in and talk. He wasn't that stupid. He realized it looked fishy for a fellow his age to be having lunch with his mother twice a week, on schedule, but he was past all that. All he knew was that she was wonderful company, much better than the quiet girl with the occasional great remark, and that was all that mattered. He called her each day, too, but kept the calls short so that the real meat of what was on his mind could be saved for the lunches.

She still had some of the old mother in her, but he found he could cut her short now whenever she started on the wrong track. That was the difference. For example, if she showed up with a new dress and stuck out her chest, saying, "What do you think of the bustline...a twenty-one-year-old girl," he would simply say, "Knock it off, mom," instead of stewing inside, the way he did when he was young and helpless. It was an important difference. On occasion, she would lecture him, giving him advice about people she didn't know. An old trick. "I don't care what you feel," she said once, in reference to one of Riegelson's colleagues, "and I admit I never met the man. But I'll bet dollars to doughnuts Wenger is out to get your job."

"But you *don't* know him, mom," he answered quite patiently, "so your advice is meaningless." And that was the end of it. Whether Wenger was indeed out to get his job was beside the point. Let's say he was. Much more important was that Riegelson was no longer helpless against his mother; he was an equal now, in his mid-thirties, and that made it an entirely different ball game. And since she could no longer hurt him, he reasoned, why not sit back and enjoy her? They could exchange dirty jokes now, and there was no sexual threat to him whatever. And she did have some pretty good insights into people, this fellow Wenger, for example, who only one person in a hundred would pick out as being sneaky. But of course his mother had never met Wenger, which is why he had to draw the line and quiet her down on the subject.

He saw his mother as a great new friend; on a trip to California, he suddenly thought why not do something nice for her and bring her out to the West Coast. In the old days, such an impulse would have been a direct capitulation to guilt, an attempt to repay her for all of "the sacrifices" that were allegedly made for him, "the way your father and I bled ourselves to send you to college." There

wasn't a trace of that feeling left in Riegelson. At one of
the lunches, he had cut her right off by saying, "Listen,
there was no sacrifice. You sent me to college because you
wanted to. It made you feel good. It was during the war
when you had the dough. In a curious way, you were the
selfish one, doing something for yourself." She listened
carefully. Amazingly, that marked the end of several de-
cades of sacrifice talk. When he was in California, Riegelson simply figured why not give the old girl a thrill, let
her tell her friends, "My son's bringing me out to Hollywood," and let her sit around the pool and soak up the
lovely weather. So he sent her a first-class ticket. He had
been fond of saying he had a hotel suite big enough to
house a large family of Puerto Ricans. After a minimum
of thought, he set it up so that she could check right in
with him for a week or two. Staying in a suite with your
mother? Big deal. Let other people worry about it. In his
heart he was as cool as a cucumber. When the bellhop
brought her bags to Riegelson's quarters, almost reflexively
she sailed into one of her old routines, asking the bellhop
if he thought they were lovers or something. Riegelson
nipped that one off right on the spot. "Look mom," he
said, "none of that. You ever pull any of that lover stuff
again, I'll send you right back on the next plane. Now
behave yourself." She lowered her head meekly like a little
girl who'd been scolded and that was the last of it. It was
a great new way he had come up with of handling her.
Lay it right on the line and get rid of it. Come to think of
it, no one had ever handled her that way before.

By this time, he had left the quiet girl. She had finally
gone over the line with her quietness and he figured out
that she wasn't quiet and reflective so much as deeply depressed. So he got out of that one. In California, he had
dates with a series of girls who were deeply involved in the
zodiac and each of whom seemed to have broken up with

boyfriends recently. None of the ones he ran into wanted to get involved in heavy scenes, either. As long as they weren't looking for anything heavy, Riegelson figured he might as well enjoy some light scenes and bum around, after hours, with his mother. He took her to a few screenings of new films and actually enjoyed the puzzlement in the eyes of the people who saw them together, a young fellow and an old lady. What was he supposed to do, be a hypocrite and take out a young girl, let her bore him to death with Taurus and Leo talk when there wasn't even a heavy scene coming up at the end of the evening? To hell with that. It was much better having a truly rich and rewarding evening with his mother who was even easier and more relaxed on the West Coast. A couple of times, he gave her hundred-dollar bills, folded up, at the end of their lunches together and told her to go wild in the stores. And did she know how to appreciate the little gifts!

Riegelson's mom had never been out of the country and for his Christmas vacation, he decided to really give her a thrill and take her to Nassau in the Bahamas. He would be able to get in a little gambling and she would have the sun and the tremendous enjoyment of taking an overseas flight. They checked into a giant double room with a large terrace facing the ocean, a setup she appreciated the way no one in the world would have been able to. Standing at the guardrails, she looked out at the breaking waves, let the thin spray go against her face and said, "If I were to close my eyes right now, I swear I'd die happy. I've finally found paradise." She cautioned him against gambling too heavily, but he took care of that one with a raised finger and a look and that was the end of that. He won quite a bit of money the third night out and amazed himself by being able to pull out of the casino with the money in hand. Maybe he felt gambling money was dirty. In any case, he had always felt compelled to give his winnings back to the casino, even if it meant staying until four in the morning. But he quit this one time at nine in the evening and met his mother in the island's finest restaurant, a candelabraed place with a lovely terraced view of the surf. She had picked up a rich tan in no time—everyone in his family had that capacity—and her figure had gone back to trim, an amazing feat for a woman her age. He was quite proud of her. The aging process had slowed up, stopped and from all appearances gone into reverse. No one would take her for a day over fifty. She had gone back to drinking, but very light stuff, Campari on the rocks, a far cry from the old straight rye and straight vodka days. He didn't comment on that. There would be plenty of time to get after her if she ever upped the ante. Meanwhile, it was great seeing her. She was kidding around with two waiters and had them in the palm of her hand. When Riegelson came over, she said, "Here comes my son. I have to behave myself now." That cracked them up. "Your mother's a pistol," said one of them. Riegelson didn't bother to pick that one up. He simply shrugged and sat down beside her. She really was a pistol, but a different kind of pistol now, one he could handle and enjoy with no fear that it would go off in his face. When he slid next to her, a Wasp-type couple looked up from their vichyssoise bowls and made disapproving faces. The hell with them, that was their problem. In the old days, Riegelson would have gotten upset and been tempted to kill the pair of them for their attitude. Now they didn't faze him in the slightest. He knew damned well that if his mother wanted to charm the couple, particularly the guy, and make him laugh, she could have done it in two seconds flat. But why bother with the sons of bitches. The important thing now was how wonderful he felt. And right in the middle of an aggravating divorce suit, that was the extraordinary part. He had twelve crisp hundred-dollar bills in casino money in his pocket.

His face was raw with a fresh suntan and after five minutes or so he felt the first easy glow of tropical drinking. He loved the way his mother looked, even the heaviness of her perfume, which in this new situation had no threat to it whatever. Her voice had a new hitch to it, something along the lines of the early Jean Arthur, and there was no way to describe it other than to call it charming. He put his arm around her, gave her a kiss on the neck and a good strong hug and decided right then and there he would take the old girl dancing later and the hell with anyone who didn't like the idea. And then he sat back and marveled at how fine he felt. And how wonderful it was, for the first time in his life, and after all those years of aggravation, to be absolutely free.

—1969.

# The
# Best
# We Have

A T A BLISSFUL TIME OF his life, staring out at the bright blue Caribbean sea, Parker felt only one small tug of regret—that his friend, Abraham Smoeller, could not be sharing his great good fortune. Parker had dashed off the libretto of a musical comedy that had become hair-raisingly successful. With companies forming in Hong Kong and far-off Upper Volta, he could easily afford lazy vacations in the sun. His friend Smoeller was another story.

Hailed, for what now seemed a fraction of a second, as a bold young prince of the American theater, Smoeller had quickly thereafter been pelted from the stage in a storm of abuse, as if his subsequent works were monstrous crimes. Licking his wounds, the dramatist had slipped off quietly to the wilds of New Jersey, to scratch out a meager though honest life as assistant professor of medieval literature at a small community college. Yet Parker knew his worth. Unashamedly, and perhaps too often, he announced to small literary groups that Smoeller was a better man than he was. "Better than all of us," he would add. "The best we have."

As the years rolled along, Parker had made efforts to help his friend—encouraging him; luring him into Manhattan for lavish dinners; even pressing money upon him which Smoeller refused, although, in truth, Parker didn't press too hard. Once in a while, like a bugle in the distance, a faint signal would be heard: "Smoeller is working." But that's all it remained—a signal.

Now, inside his sumptuous villa, Parker's third wife—a beauty, and the first with waist-length hair—happily hummed away as she washed his clothing in Woolite, an absurd economy in light of his present circumstances, yet one more sign of his trouble-free existence. On the balcony, Parker sleepily regarded two coconuts high in a tree, wondering—if his life depended on it—whether he would be able to shin his way up and knock at least one loose. In this mood, he hatched a vague plan to help his forgotten friend.

Back in Manhattan, Parker called Petrussian, editor of a powerful biweekly—its support for a play of intellectual striving was usually enough to tilt the balance in its favor. Once a literary enemy, Petrussian, possibly attracted by the glitter of Parker's new success, had recently sent out a peace feeler. The two former antagonists met for lunch at a Ukrainian restaurant, Petrussian's favorite, and casually talked of such matters as cultural grants and the regional theater.

On occasion, while its regular man sojourned abroad, Petrussian's magazine took on guest critics. Parker, with time on his hands, hinted that he might be available for just such a vacancy. In response, Petrussian curled his upper lip, reminding Parker of the old wound. Years back, in a cowardly attack, Petrussian had described Parker in print as a poseur, a man who had never written a single word that absolutely had to be written. He hadn't even had the grace to allow Parker to respond. As the memory returned, Parker felt like grabbing him by the throat. Instead, he shifted the conversation to Ibsen revivals and drank glass after glass of tea—no mean feat. A week later, Petrussian called, asking for house seats to Parker's smash musical—and offering him the fall.

With impish delight, or at least the closest he had ever come to that state, Parker called his old friend, once again luring him into the city with the promise of a sumptuous dinner at a four star restaurant. Who knows, Parker thought suddenly, perhaps he always joins me out of simple friendship.

It had been months since Parker had seen the brilliant dramatist and he was amazed at how frail his friend had become. Clumps of hair had disappeared. The great Smoeller, who had once sported a monocle and walked with the swagger of a cuirassier, now stumbled along at the edge of old age.

It broke Parker's heart to see his friend in this state. Clearly, lesser minds were responsible. Yet never once did Abraham Smoeller lash out at his detractors. Quietly, in a dignified manner, he had gone about his business, piecing together a life of humble scholarship. Never mind; Parker would correct this injustice.

The two old friends embraced; and, after wine and an appetizer, Parker broke the news.

"You once suggested I do criticism," he said. "All right, now I'm doing it."

In response, Smoeller lifted his head for one reflective moment, then patted Parker's wrist gently and ordered duck à l'orange. Throughout the meal, that single pat on the wrist would stand as Smoeller's only acknowledgment of the potentially momentous importance to him of Parker's appointment. Parker, as well, pushed discretion to new heights by never once suggesting that the two men had entered into so much as a tacit agreement. Only as they hailed cabs did Parker venture to ask his friend if he happened to be working on anything.

"A few scenes," said Smoeller, spotting a Checker.

"Wonderful," said Parker, clasping Smoeller's thin bones. "That's the best news I've heard in years."

Parker greeted the arrival of fall by plunging into his new work, taking on whatever the theater had to throw at him—lightweight musicals, fluffier than his own; cries of anguish from the spiritually disfranchised; and experimental pieces. One of these particularly stuck in his craw; it featured actors exchanging philosophies while "fishing"

above the footlights with imaginary trout lines. In the plays
he reviewed, all matters of significance occurred offstage.
The news of Joan of Arc's martyrdom arrived via messen-
ger. The Bastille was stormed in the wings.

When winter approached, with not so much as a peep
out of Smoeller, it seemed the plan would crumble. Parker
thought of calling the dramatist to ask how he was coming
along, but decided this would be rude. Then, at October's
end, the gods winked down—if not upon Parker himself,
then at least upon his scheme. Petrussian's regular critic,
without so much as a notice to the publication that had
made him famous, simply waltzed off to join a Bulgarian
film company as a consultant. Petrussian had made no
effort to conceal his pleasant surprise at the depths of
Parker's acerbity; who knows, perhaps he was in a bind.
Whatever the case, he offered Parker the job, full-time.

Parker was of two minds about this. On the one hand,
he felt a need to go back to his work—yet another idea
for a lightweight musical had occurred to him, more surefire than the last; also, what if Smoeller never produced
anything and simply marched to his grave in silence? Where
would that leave Parker? Yet, on the other hand, fierce
loyalty to his friend left him no choice.

"I'll take it," he told Petrussian, who had the gall to curl
his lip again. "But I don't know how long I can last. It's
wearing." Not simultaneously, but a week later, news of a
stupendous nature reached Parker in a coffee shop:
Smoeller had completed a draft.

Parker, who would have gladly settled for an act, re-
joiced. Fortified by his friend's impending return to the
theater, his work became more tolerable. Watching a lightweight review, an overpraised British import, an all-gay
version of *Coriolanus,* he would silently address the restless
audience. "Wait," he would tell them. "Soon you'll see a

playwright. Soon you'll watch a play." And soon they did. Smoeller's new work was modestly heralded by a small item in the local press. *MacMahon* by Abraham Smoeller would be presented in mid-December. No stars were listed; and, as far as Parker was concerned, none were needed. Stars in his early work had done some of the damage. Smoeller's wit, the sweep and pageantry of his touch, would get the job done. The producing company was a relatively obscure one, known primarily for the scrupulous attention to detail it had paid to the works of Arthur Wing Pinero. How nice to know that its place in dramatic literature would soon be assured. The theater was a two-hundred seater, but this, too, was unimportant. Could any theater, whatever its size, truly contain a vigorous new work by Abraham Smoeller?

As the day of the opening approached, Parker suddenly feared that Petrussian, sensing the connection between the two old friends, would ask him to stand aside in place of a neutral observer. The son of a bitch actually did seem to be toying with the idea, sadistically asking Parker to drop round the office for no good reason and looking at him in a funny way. Parker dressed quickly on opening night and bolted to the theater, lest a last-minute edict arrive from the wily Armenian. As he took his seat on the shabby aisle, he felt an urge to indulge himself in a single sly wink, and looked around for Smoeller. But the great dramatist was nowhere to be found; possibly he was sitting in a bar nearby, understandably the victim of opening-night jitters.

When Parker had read the title of the play—*Mac-Mahon*—he had assumed, correctly, as it turned out, that the play dealt with the French general whose failure to relieve nineteenth-century Sedan had led to humiliating defeat at the hands of the Prussians. This pleased Parker enormously; it promised scenes of sweep and grandeur—in other words, Smoeller country.

The play began somewhat curiously, with MacMahon whimpering in his tent, the sounds of battle in the distance. A classically traditional chorus appeared quickly, describing the fate that awaited the doomed general; then, for no apparent reason, a second chorus, all black, entered, taunting the first chorus in a jeering street style: "You ain't no chorus. You can't even sing." Both groupings were then hoisted into the wings, making way for a crudely inserted and interminable romance between MacMahon and a Sedanese shopgirl. Act One ended with MacMahon back in his tent, whimpering.

At first, Parker had been puzzled, then confused. At the end of the act, he was in shock and raced to the refreshment counter where, unfortunately, only punch was served. Was it possible that he had missed something? Had Smoeller deliberately set up a string of inane scenes to make some point about a disordered universe? Could it be that he was deliberately digging himself into a dramatic hole so that he could dig himself out, the better to demonstrate his genius? If so, he had better get going.

Act Two, Parker was relieved to see, began more promisingly, with MacMahon lecturing at length on the capabilities of the breech-loading *chassepot*. With some discomfort, however, Parker began to feel that this was an entirely different MacMahon, one who delivered his soliloquy incomprehensibly, in a wisecracking Broadway style. Was it possible that the new MacMahon was left over from an early draft? Actually, it didn't matter—both MacMahons were reprehensible. Maddeningly, the choruses reappeared for a bout of endless squabbling, their place taken by an inconsequential ball at Versailles. The action, such as it was, eventually returned to MacMahon's tent with the general bent over his desk, his final whimpers capped off by a howl of anguish at the curtain.

Parker heard vague sounds of applause, but he was not

the man to gauge the audience's reaction. He only knew his own—stupefaction. What he had seen was an outright disaster. What would he do now? Resign? The time to have done that was before the opening; he could just imagine Petrussian's expression if he pleaded a nepotistic connection at this late date and refused to turn in a review. The only honorable course was to proceed. Smoeller himself would support that view. Fortunately, he had a long deadline. There was time to cast about for some small shard of excellence in the work. The word *vessel* was his solution; in his return to the theater, Abraham Smoeller had come up with a great vessel for a play. Having made that observation, Parker had no choice but to point out that the vessel was shot through with holes and should never have been put out to sea.

Patiently and very methodically, as Smoeller would have wanted him to do, Parker ticked off the play's innumerable flaws. Never once failing to engage the work on its own terms, he left it for dead. In a desperate attempt to end on a positive note, he praised the leader of the black chorus as a young man with a long career in front of him. Then, sadly and dutifully, he filed his review.

The following day, Parker was surprised at how charitable the other reviewers had been. Although some had mixed feelings, one called the play "ambitious," another "bold and complex." A third headlined his notice, "Welcome Back, Abraham Smoeller." The play hung on the edge, awaiting Parker's evaluation; there was no question that a cannonade of praise from the respected biweekly might very well have put it over the top, ensuring a respectable run, perhaps a lucrative film sale. But then, the savage Parker denunciation appeared. The play tottered for a bit; and, after seven previews and fourteen performances, it quietly expired.

Although Parker was heartsick, never once did he regret

his action. What if the play had continued, night after night disgracing Smoeller's triumphant, though admittedly unappreciated, early work? How would that have made Parker feel? How would that have made Smoeller feel? The only bump in the road for Parker was that eventually he would have to face his friend. He thought of calling him, dropping him a note, but what, finally, could he say that his review didn't convey?

One day, in late December, he ran into Smoeller unexpectedly in a noisy Chelsea cafeteria. As he leaned over to pay for a fruit salad, the dramatist, if possible, seemed even more decrepit than he had before. He saw Parker, and approached him unsteadily. For an instant, it seemed he was about to rise up to his old dashing height and cleave Parker in two. Instead, he tapped his arm gently as if to say, "I know. And it's all right." The gesture produced a rush of emotion in Parker, who threw his arms around the other man. "But you've got to continue," he told Smoeller, his tears wetting his old friend's shoulders. "You're all we've got. You're the last hope of the American theater."

—1983.

# The
# Car Lover

A| ONE-ACT PLAY with two characters: BUYER, in his mid-thirties; SELLER, somewhat older. The scene is an auto leasing office, in the late afternoon. There is a massive frame of car, great-mouthed, blinding in its chromium magnificence; a steel animal.

BUYER *(admiring car)*: It really is great. I didn't think I was one of those guys, but it stopped me dead on the street. I saw two of them, in the same color. Both times I just stood there and sucked in my breath. I think I saluted or something.

SELLER: It's going to be a tremenjus seller. Tremenjus.

BUYER: And cars don't usually do that to me. I'm not one of those car freaks. You know, out in the back, tinkering with the old flivver. Gee, dad, can I take her for a spin. I have a friend who actually became a fag for an Alfa Romeo. A producer's son promised him one. He said, "I'll give you an Alfa Romeo if you come up to my hotel room and pretend you're my older brother, give me a bath and stuff." My friend shot right up to the hotel room, didn't bat an eyelash.

SELLER: Some fellas'll do anything, won't they.

BUYER: But I'm not one of those guys. It's just *this* car. The way this one is. It's amazing, it's just a machine and look at the way I'm carrying on. I've heard about that. Getting horny for a car, just as though it were a girl. Well, there's no use denying it. I'm horny for this one. And I'm not one of those guys.

SELLER: Well, then, let's draw it up, shall we. You know, it's all deductible. We write you a letter saying it's garaged in the country and used for business purposes. You can write the whole thing off. Uncle Sam picks up the tab. Uncle Samerooney.

BUYER: I don't even think it's a sex-symbol deal either. You know, an inadequate fellow and here he gets a giant phallus to drive around in. I honestly don't think it's that.

SELLER: I don't think it's that either.

BUYER: Maybe it's the color. I've seen blues, but never this one. It's got to be a new blue that no one's ever heard of before. A breakthrough in blues. What do they call it?

SELLER: Royal Monarch Blue.

BUYER: It's that blue that's pressing certain buttons in me, certain subliminal blue buttons I don't even know about. They probably had an army of research people who came up with that blue and knew it would go right to work on these blue buttons inside of me.

SELLER: It's a helluva blue.

BUYER: I don't care what's doing it to me. Good Christ, I really love this car. I wish there were a way to convey it to you. I could just eat up this car. I could just chew off a piece and swallow it down. Like a chocolate mousse, a new dessert I've recently become fond of.... It's amazing... I haven't even been *in* the damned thing yet.

SELLER: Would you like that? Go ahead, feller. Jump in. You can drive it around if you like.

BUYER: I don't have to. I know what it's going to be like in there. I know about the quiet of it and the smell. I know about the royal way I'm going to feel. I know how my posture will be in there, a new kind of royal posture. I don't even know that much about cars. But I know about this one. The smoothness of it. The quiet. It's one of those things. I'll go in there—it's a hard thing to pass up—but I know what I'm going to find.

SELLER: Go ahead.

BUYER *jumps in and then comes out after a few minutes.*

BUYER: I don't even want to talk about it. I just want to

stand here and let it cling to me. Bathe in it. It was a whole
religious experience. A Zen thing. I could hardly even
breathe. I didn't want to spoil anything. Good Christ, what
a car.

SELLER: It's the best there is. The best your almighty buck
can buy.

BUYER: There's one thing. It's almost moronic to bring
it up. Just pretend you didn't hear it when I say it, but I
have to anyway. When I make this small criticism, it'll make
my enthusiasm seem all the more rich.

SELLER: Say it. Go ahead. Get it off your chest.

BUYER: The visibility isn't that great.

SELLER: You get used to that. Around ten minutes after
you start driving. And when you do, it becomes a plus.
Keeps you on your toes. One of the best things about the
car.

BUYER: I'm sorry I even brought the damned thing up.
I feel like an ass.

SELLER: You had to relieve it from your chest. Now let's
write it up. I've got a lot of it already. Name...address...I've
got your phone...I need a bank reference.

BUYER: Chase Manhattan....My wife really needles me
about it. About going out to buy this particular type of car.
When I'd always been sworn to their destruction. It's just
that they never really made a car until they made this
model. Boy, does she needle me. They say that's good,
though. Takes the pressure out of a marriage. They found
that out about atomic submarines, too. The ones that take
those two-month underwater cruises. It's good to have a
few needlers along to break the pressure. Annie really
sticks it in there, though. Once I accidentally threw a dart
in her shoulder. Up in Lake George. Couple of tetanus
shots and she was as good as new. But she's needled me
about that for years.

SELLER: They all do. And it builds up, too, over the years.

I myself think a divorce should be full of hatred, where you really want to kill each other. You do something lousy to each other, spit in each other's face, get a divorce and then keep it that way. Anything else is just dawdling, hanging on the fence. Anything else is just farting around.

BUYER: I don't see it that way. I think it ought to be a lot friendlier.

SELLER: I don't. I think it ought to have some clear-cut hate in it. So a man knows where he stands with the bitch....Let's see....You've never leased before...you probably don't know that we take care of everything. Parts. Maintenance. Say you're visiting your little tykes up in Rhode Island somewhere and you crack a fan belt. Slap on a new fan belt, send us the bill and back you go to your tykes.

BUYER: I don't happen to have any tykes. But I know what you mean.

SELLER: It's a clean operation. All you pay for is gas and oil. We send you a letter and the government pays for the whole package. Courtesy of Uncle Samerooney.

BUYER: I can't believe I'm going to own it. I think it's the proudness of it that gets me. The proud lines. It's like an entire country, a newly emerging one, full of all this pride.

SELLER: I know what you mean. Now you take old Shirley Ferris—that's a guy; I think he sits on twenty corporations and that's the name they hung on him—anyway, he calls me the other day, unusual thing, and he's shaking like a leaf, right over the phone. The man sits on twenty corporations. "Oakie," he says, "they swiped my car right out of the garage. What am I going to do, Oakie." And then he starts to boohoo. I say to him, "Didn't you lock it up, Shirley," and he says, "I don't know, Oakie. All I know is they swiped it out of here and I don't have my car." And then he really cuts loose, bawling his head off. For Christ's sakes, the man sits on twenty corporations.

BUYER: I can see that. I can see why he'd feel that way.

SELLER: I said to him, "Shirl, I'll have another car over to you by five tonight." We do that, part of the deal. "Just make sure you phone it in to the precinct."

BUYER: I should think you'd get it back. Where would you go with a car like that? It would be like trying to hide the Verrazano Bridge. Anyway, I can understand both sides of it. I can see him crying and I can see some person wanting to steal it. I'd steal it myself.

SELLER: Anyway, here comes the unusual part. I calm Shirley down and it isn't two hours before I get a call from an officer named Monaghan in the 13th Precinct. "You lose a car?" he asks. "Yeah," I said. "I got it," he says. What happened is he was driving his scooter through the park and he sees this sedan go off the highway and nick the edge of a tree. He goes over to the car—amazing, it's Shirley Ferris' car—the door opens and this little spick jumps outside and disappears in the bushes. A shitty little spick, couldn't have been this high. They couldn't grab him. Monaghan says he must have been greased up or something. Anyway, we got the car back for old Shirley and it was like giving a kid a surprise party. And then he comes in with his punch line. "Oakie," he says, "could you have the Police Department deliver my car to the office tonight." Well, after I quit laughing—I almost busted my gut—I said, "Well now, Shirley, that's the only thing we can't do for you under this lease arrangement. We can't get the Police Department to make a personal delivery of your car." And it is, you know. It's the only thing we can't pull off. But we do everything else for you and you know who picks up the tab. *(Salutes patriotically and sings:)* ... and the rockets' red glare....

BUYER: What'd you have to say that for?

SELLER: What's that?

BUYER: Little spick. Why did you say that?

SELLER: What do you mean? He was a little spick. I don't get your meaning.

BUYER: You shouldn't have said that. I'm in here leasing a car from you and you shouldn't have said that. There are some people who would've said that and others who wouldn't. And you did.

SELLER: You involved with spicks?

BUYER: I'm not involved with anybody. You think just because I'm in here buying a car, because I made some extra money. You think just because I love that car with all my heart that you can say spick.

SELLER: It was part of a goddamned story. To make my point. About how we do everything. Lubrication. Tires. We change the filters. You need a new fan belt you got it. What do I care about spicks. There's not a spick around for miles.... You're not a spick, are you?

BUYER: No, I'm not a spick.

SELLER: I didn't think so. I thought you might have had a little spick in you—maybe on your grandma's side—and I came along and frayed your nerves. But I could tell you weren't straight spick.

BUYER: Maybe it's just the timing. I got a shine from a colored guy this morning. He told me I had to take my shoes off. Because never in his life had he ever shined a pair of shoes on a man's foot. He's shined thousands of pairs—starting out in Jackson someplace—but even down there you had to take them off or he wouldn't touch your shoes. He was an old guy with fingers on him like I'd never seen before—big, floating, water-filled ones, as though they'd been run through a special kind of press for colored guys. To get a license—if you're a colored guy—you have to put your fingers in this press and get them stamped. Anyway, I knew that if I offered him a thousand dollars to shine my shoes without my taking them off, he would've turned it down.

SELLER: I thought we were talking spicks.

BUYER: I was tempted to. I'm no angel—I made a little money—and I was tempted to write out a check for a grand to see if I could get him to do it. He wouldn't have, though. I knew it. Off-the-feet was his way. I took off my shoes and stood there in my socks and he took them over to the side and shined them and I almost died.

SELLER: I still don't get the connection.

BUYER: I'll tell you what. Maybe you'll get this. (*Rips off piece of car.*) You know, I really ought to whip your ass for what you did. I ought to tear your head off, you bloody sonofabitch. You thought you had a customer, didn't you. I'll give you spicks. (*Demonstrating:*) Why don't I just run your head under these double-ply tubeless four-frame optional sidewalls. Would you like that? Maybe I'll just burn your eyes out with these double-gauge, adjustable, swivel-beamed, reflecting illuminators. Two guys, friendly, folksy, making a little deal, throw in a few spicks to make things cozy. I'll give you a deal....

SELLER: You're out of your mind.

BUYER: Wait a minute. I have an idea. Come in here. (*Drags* SELLER *inside car.*) I think I'll just crack your head a little in these generously padded, double-weight, safety-recessed doors, you mother. Would you go for that. I mean what if I just sliced your ass a little in these conveniently located power-vent electrically operated windows. Would you love that. (*Drags* SELLER *outside again.*) I'll give you spicks. What'd you call him? Shitty little spick. Here, let me just tie your head onto these three-speed, glare-reducing wiper arms with their four handy jet-washer streams. There y'are. Go. (BUYER *props* SELLER *on hood of car, head attached to wiper arms, going back and forth with them, splashed intermittently by washers.*) You love it? (BUYER *finally turns off wipers, allows* SELLER *to collect himself, climb down.*) Pig. Thought you had me there. Throw in a few spicks to nail down the deal. All right, now I'm going to teach you a lesson. You can stop your writing. I'll get the goddamned car somewhere else. You crud. I wouldn't spit on the worst part of you.

SELLER: You're out of your mind. I could see if I'd insulted your particular nationality. Maybe you'd have a beef. What the hell do I care about spicks? I was telling a goddamned anecdotal story.

BUYER: Shove it up your speedway.

SELLER: I happen to think you've got a screw loose, young man. *(He is much more composed.)* You know, I could make a phone call now. I'm not saying that I am. But I could. They don't make many of these cars, you know. This particular model. I could make a phone call and see to it that you don't get one anywhere. I could close out every dealer in the East. If I wanted to.

BUYER: I'd like to see you make a phone call like that. Go ahead. That's something I'd love to see.

SELLER: I'm not saying that I am. Just that I could. I could wait till you leave and then do it. And you'd never have that car. You'd never get to be inside it and drive it. Feel it respond under your touch on the open road. Unless you wanted to wait a year and buy a used-up piece of crap.

BUYER *(with ever so slightly less conviction)*: You shouldn't have said spick. You shouldn't have taken it for granted that just because I love that car, because I want it as much as I do, that you could say anything.

SELLER *(shuffling papers)*: Right. Now it's late. I got some things to clean up.

BUYER *(starting to leave, then hesitating)*: Where were you brought up? Probably around the old Hell's Kitchen area, I would guess.

SELLER *(occupied)*: No. Nowhere like that. Someplace near there, but not there.

BUYER: You probably had trouble with the Spanish

people, right? You'd been living there for years, *your* neighborhood, *your* stores—and all of a sudden there was an invasion, a new culture, threatening your jobs, what you thought was a threat to your women—your livelihood. So there was this natural resentment, right?

SELLER: We didn't have that at all. We had it with the Polacks. I never saw a spick. Till I was around thirty. They started coming in around then.

BUYER *(not hearing)*: Sometimes it got violent. I know how it must have been. One of the Spanish people drops a cement bag—from a rooftop—right on one of your women, kills her. A teenage girl. The worst thing imaginable—something dragged out of a nightmare. There's a funeral, and the next day your people retaliate. You go out with bats and kill three of what you feel are the enemy. You bat them to death in an alley. And all this hate goes into your blood. Gradually, as the years pass along, there's a truce, something you can live with, maybe even a few intermarriages. It all gets filmed over. Isn't that the way it was?

SELLER *(deliberately)*: No. Nothing like that. We never had no spicks. We never heard of them, didn't know what they were. Now that's just the way it was. You want the car?

BUYER: The scars go very deep. They go right into the tissue and bone of your life. It's something you can't help. And every once in a while, it comes out. A gesture. A phrase. *Spick*. An echo of that rooftop cement bag and that teenage girl on the pavement. Isn't that what happens?

SELLER *(after a long pause, with irony)*: Sure. That's what happens. Now where did you say your house was mortgaged? I have to have that.

BUYER: Morgan Trust. Albany, New York....It's practically a reflex, something you can't help.

SELLER: How long have you been at the same address?

BUYER: Two years, two and a half. *Spick*. It might as well be a tic or a hiccup for all it means. *(Turning to car.)* I wonder what it is about this car. It's not even a sexual thing. Maybe it is. I think it's the proud part. It's the first one I've ever seen where they worked the proudness right into the metal, right into the construction. I really love this car.

—1968.

# Our Lady
# of the
# Lockers

**T**HEY FOUND HER BODY IN locker three hundred fifty-seven at Jack La Lanne's Gym and Health Spa on East Fifty-fifth Street. Also in lockers three hundred fifty-eight through three hundred sixty-one. I heard about it on a small island off the South Carolina coast where I was failing to enjoy my first vacation in five years. The highlight of my social activity (not including a little something with the girl at the desk) was a barroom conversation with a stock broker who spent a great deal of time telling me why he would not go to Elaine's restaurant in New York. He could name me fifteen places that served better pasta. He was not too happy with the way they prepared their drinks. He wanted to know why he should go there and get shoved around by the waiters when the city was bursting with places that treated you with a little courtesy. The celebrities? He knew plenty of them. He was in petrodollars. Kevin McCarthy had once crossed the full length of the Russian Tea Room just to shake his hand. Who in Christ's name, he wanted to know, did Elaine think she was, making him wait an hour and a half for a table? As far as he was concerned, the restaurant was just another overrated hash house that he would not be caught dead in.

I listened to quite a bit of this and then I suggested that maybe he ought to simply put Elaine's out of his mind and go about his business.

He ordered a double something or other, took a long pull on it, and said, "Goddamned good idea."

The story made the island *Bugle*. The body was in an awful lot of lockers, so it was a little tough to work with, but they got a positive I.D. on the girl from her dental markings. A show-biz dentist had done her bite in a distinctive manner. He was very much in vogue a few years back and had done the bites of the entire El Morocco crowd. Also, girls who worked in boutiques. Any girl named Danielle was sure to have had her bite done by this fellow. He did a lot of Nicoles, too. What he did was to sculpt the surfaces of the biter's teeth in a decorative manner that, not incidentally, produced an erotic sensation of screaming intensity in anyone lucky enough to be the bitee. It also enabled the biter to gnaw holes in Gucci belts that needed to be taken in after crash diets, and, in an emergency, to kill small animals. He did the upper right side of my mouth. So I am an expert on this fellow—since I have been both a bitee and twenty-five percent of a biter. I'll say more about this later—if you're good.

The paper that came in from the mainland was a bit more ambitious and got into blood drops, which, according to one source, pointed almost like an arrow to the Health Spa sauna. This told me that Gumm was the duty detective on the case. Whenever a homicide involved a considerable shedding of blood, he always wanted to know exactly which way the drops pointed. To my knowledge, this has never led to the apprehension of a murderer, or even a suspect, but he stays involved with them. In the old days, when we had humor in the department, we would have referred to this interest of his as Gumm Drops. However, we don't do humor anymore. We have left that to the Adam-12s and the Kojaks. It's probably a good thing, because we were never that funny. Neither are the networks, but they are better than we ever were.

Since my throat got bitten, I've had the phone set up so that no one can get through to me at night. I absolutely have to have eight good hours or I'm a lox. That's the only thing left over from the throat bite. The department understands and has decided to put up with it. If something broke, for example, on my dildo thing (an assault case I'm involved with), the department would send someone over to bang on my door. On the dildo matter, I'm not being cute. If you had seen the damage it had done to a Long Island Rail Road porter's face, you would know what I mean. It was loaded up with something heavy, but it was a dildo and that's how the unknown assaulter wanted to get the job done. Go argue with him. It's one of my unsolved cases, but I don't lose any sleep over it. I'll get it done. It's sort of on the back burner.

As I lay abed on my charming, albeit boring, island off the Carolina coast, Gumm broke through my elaborate protective phone device and buzzed me awake at four in the morning. He was failing to respect the aftermath of my throat injury, which I thought was unfeeling of him, although I did not comment on his rudeness at the time. He told me about the blood drops, of course. He said the emergency unit high-intensity lights had broken down and they didn't have such hot pictures. But they did have a breast with some saliva that would or might give them the blood type of the certain someone with whom they had a bone to pick. And they also had Jack La Lanne's Gym and Health Spa membership list, which included, among the noteworthies, writers of the feminist persuasion, Lubovitcher rabbis and a good many Israelis who quarreled heatedly with the Lubovitcher fellows in the whirlpool bath. I sensed that this was not going to be a factor in the solution of the high crime in question, but I let Gumm go on about it, thinking what the hell, in our industry (as in Charlton Heston's) you never know. Once Gumm had played out his Lubovitcher material, I decided, if not to pounce on him, then at least to take him to task on his rudeness.

"I am on vacation, Gumm," I said, not invoking the issue of whether I was having a good time, since it is not my way to push my sorrows off on other people, as I wish they would not push theirs off on me. "And yet you call me in the darkness of the night and disturb my rest. Why?"

"I am glad you brought that up," said my colleague, the famed blood-drops man. "We searched the young lady's apartment and came across a pile of tape recordings. It was her style to tape her male callers, lovers and otherwise. Some were named Jean Claude, others Jean Pierre. And there was one fellow—let's not beat around the bush— who turned out to be you. My question, therefore..."

"I am not now, never have been nor will I ever be a suspect in this case."

"Thank you, Herbert, and I am sorry to have had to be so blunt and pushy."

"That's perfectly all right."

We exchanged good-byes, and since I had been totally forthright with my friend, I was able to turn over and fade back into the sleep of the just.

The next morning, before setting sail for the Big Apple, I had myself an O.J., two croissants and a cup of coffee, all of it crawling with cholesterol. You could practically see the cholesterol swimming around in it, but what the hell, it was my last day of fun in the sun, so why stand on ceremony.

I positioned myself in the Cafeteria à la Tropicana, so that I would be sitting casually yet not conspicuously next to the fellow with the attraction-repulsion thing about Elaine's. He tried to rope me into some breakfast conversation with an anecdote about how Henri Soulé had opened Pavillon just to spite Harry Cohn, but I didn't go for it. He had material on Clarke's, "21" and even the old Stork Club, all involving guys who would not set foot in them on the ground of honor, but not one nibble did he get from me. My objective was to get another look at him and fix him in my mind. Overnight, he had become a little

vague. And after all, he had approached me, uninvited
...and it was just the two of us in this el weirdo hotel. In
my business it is no handicap to walk around with a nice,
robust sense of paranoia. It had always been my view that
they should have lowered the height requirement years
ago and let in guys with what I just said.

In a somewhat different spirit, I paid a farewell visit to
the girl behind the desk. There is a certain something that
comes over me when I am alone with girls in offices, a
kind of clerical horniness. My Air Force commanding officer, a South Carolina man, would have explained it thusly:
"Don't you see, Barker, it's the very *absence* of anything
hoaney in an office that's makin' you so hoaney." He had
been able to prove, in this manner, that The New Yorker
was the world's most erotic magazine. "No question about
it, The New Yoakeh tebbly hoaney, the hoaniest publication
in all journalism." Whatever the case, the desk girl and I
had our farewell congress in the accounting department;
when it came time to sign the bill, I saw that the little rascal
had completely forgotten to add on the tax, a not incon-
siderable saving to your correspondent of sixty-five much-
needed little ones.

A word about Our Lady of the Lockers. Her name was
Crystal. All but the least discerning of readers will have
noted a certain wry, offhanded *je ne sais quoi* tone in the
style of these jottings; consult any Central Park West shrink
worth his—what is it now?—$60 a pop and he will tell you
that this is a defense against the tenderness of the subject.
And he will be on target. My feelings for Crystal were
strong. I loved Crystal. As to her name, I do not wish to
do battle on behalf of it. It was as Crystal that she appeared
to me. As Crystal, I accepted her. I looked at it this way.
She might have been named Misty.

Later, of course, there would be the Jean Claudes and

Jean Pierres, but when I first met her there were gyne-
cologists and stock brokers. She appeared at the precinct
with a complaint that a gynecologist was threatening her
and would not give back her couch. At first, I thought this
was a reference to some freaky new birth-control device.
But she meant couch, as in Bloomingdale's furniture department. Normally, I would have had a question or two
to ask her, since obviously there were holes in this story.
But Crystal had spent several of her formative years in
Calcutta; as a result, her story, in its delivery, took on a
Higher Logic. Of *course* a mean gynecologist was threatening her and refused to part with her couch. So I agreed
to pay the gyno a visit. Understand quickly that a visit from
one of us fellows is not one of your basic social calls. And
it is not the gun that adds sauce to these visits of ours.
(Except for the butt, I myself am extremely reluctant to
bring my gun into play. Had my attitude been otherwise,
I would not have incurred my throat bite.) Whatever the
case, we have refined the "little visit" to a high art. The
gyno, sweating profusely, relinquished the couch and
promised to be good. (Despite an incipient case of em-
physema, he had been doing a little telephone breathing,
too, which I didn't know about. He promised to stop that,
too.) Whereupon Crystal, drawing once again upon her
Eastern background, made me see with perfect clarity why
I should use a police emergency truck to deliver said couch
to her East Side digs. From the time Peter Stuyvesant first
strolled the mud paths of Gotham, this has been a violation
of departmental regulations.

I did not move in with Crystal. She did not move in with
me. We cut it down the middle, her living with me a little,
me living with her a little, no one firmly living with anyone,
which finally got Crystal, of all people, irritated. This struck
me as being ironic, since the young wench, as the astute
reader no doubt has gathered, was not one of your stan-

dard cop-type girl friends. Or perhaps the astute reader
has not no doubt gathered it. Crystal came to our Americas
courtesy of the Swedish embassy, Thailand, Guam, Rio, a
cooking school in Brest—and other points too numerous
to mention in all but a Dickensian effort. As a child, she
had been hidden on trains, smuggled through border
checkpoints, kidnapped by right-wing uncles. Her face was
vintage Continental Heart-Stopper. Her body was tall and
still growing. She was the only woman I have ever met who
was past twenty-one and getting taller. "Do you like erot-
icism, Herbert?" she asked, after the couch was in.

"Oh, I guess I could get into a little of that."

Whereupon I made my basic reflexive headlong dive for
her labia minora (majora? I forget—whichever was closer).
She told me to relax and went to work with fruit, feathers,
a needle and thread, and some moves taught to her by a
Bangladesh Sufi who was known as "the Picasso of the
Pelvis."

She had made a detailed study of nerves, pressure points,
veins, and whatever else it is one studies when one has
determination, a lot of time on one's hands and wants to
find out everything there is to know about whatever it is
one calls the male member. One hopes one comprehends.
"Look, look," she would say, excitedly. "Look how he stands
up. Look how curious he is."

And I would look.

Why then, the reader with normal curiosity will have a
need to ponder, would this lustrous creature take more
than a casual interest in a New York City detective? A
personable enough young fellow, but—examined with cold
eyes—not one of overpowering appeal. Crystal, though no
stranger to Dresden, Port Said, the Tour d'Argent and
little jade shops in Bangkok, was new in town. Remember,
this was before the Jean Claudes and Jean Pierres. She had
put into the city after a period in La Jolla, some months

in upstate New York and a mysterious trip to the famed
Iowa State Writer's Conference. Whatever the nature of
her transaction with the gyno, she had dispatched it quickly.
And then there was me. I can only speculate that I fit
into some weirdo New York-romantic-detectivey-Singin'-in-
the-Rain fantasy of hers. (She was a bubble-gum chewin'
popcorn-swallowin' eyeball-poppin' cinema freak.) Or who
knows, maybe the kid really liked me. I am often complimented on my "dead eyes."

We filled up four and a half months like nobody's business. (It is generally the ladies who keep track of such
things, i.e., "I went with Sven for ninety-two days." Observe
that, in this case, it was your faithful correspondent.) It
meant a lot to me even if it did begin to screw up my
investigative rhythm—once l'affaire grew bumpy. And can
you imagine why the crazy wench wanted to break up?
Because she wanted me to move in with her. Permanently.
Or her to move in with me. Consider that for a moment.
*Her* move in with *me*. And here comes the clincher. *And
take care of her.* On detective's pay yet. (Admittedly, she was
multilingual, and did offer to work with the Gabon dele-
gation at the U.N.)

In any case, she was proposing a crazy mismatch. Harry
and Ben's Delicatessen taking care of the Four Seasons.
Some kid from Dalton going one-on-one with Earl the
Pearl, then facing Catfish Hunter. I mean, come off it. I
was over my head the first minute she came into the station
and offered me a Godiva mint. (How I yearned for a second one.) So I said no and she took it poorly. She stood
me up a lot. She stranded me in the lobby with two tickets
to the Ukrainian National Folk Dance Festival, which you
can imagine how desperately I wanted to see. Or how about
my solo act at Pearl's with Eugenia Sheppard's entire Saturday column, in the flesh, staring at me. (I waited two
hours and finally told Pearl to proceed with the lemon

chicken.) And then Crystal apparently grew bored and became what I probably interrupted her from becoming —the number-one Big-Time Delicious-Terrific Super Bowl of a girl of which there is only one a year (they come in around soft-shell crab time). Halston-to-Dali-to-Gernreich-to-Warhol, over to Evans-to-Stark-to-Ransohoff, shift one, two, three and so on to the Jean Claudes and Jean Pierres, which is where I lost track. And would you believe, right in the middle of this merry-go-round of coke and class, the little rascal (growing in ballsiness as well as height, I might add) would have the temerity to excuse herself from, say, a Stones concert and call Old Faithful here for "a little pin money." And I would come up with it, too, on one occasion sacrificing a new holster I had my eye on. Because I still loved her. She had taught me to take my shoes off in my apartment. She once bought me the most fantastic set of trains a man ever dreamed of, the kind I'd stop and look at in windows and figure only Getty nephews ever got to have. (It wasn't even my birthday—and you can be sure I didn't ask where she got the money.) She whispered erotic tidbits in my ear, rendering them in a perfect Liv Ullmann delivery that would have fooled the great Bergmann himself. She never once broke rhythm or sequence in bed, even when I had taken an outrageously wrong turn, obvious to the two of us; she made love to my feet, ignoring a GI injury incurred on Pork Chop Hill during that boring Korean fracas; except for the one time she almost O.D.'d on Chicken Pakora at Gaylord's, she always smelled Tahitian; she greeted each day with a smile. She got my bite fixed (just the upper right, as it turned out, due to a falling out with Dr. Wen over my Detective's Dental Plan). Not so deep in the recesses of my thinking, I figured that after all the Jean Claudes and Jean Pierres, who knows, maybe she just might...but now she was in all those lockers, and I was on my way back to New York City, scene of the crime, although, frankly, I was not going directly to either La Lanne's or the Bureau. First I had to get out my dry cleaning and check my plants. I figured I would sort of ease into it.

My senses sharpened as I crossed Sixth Avenue. "I guess you can always tell a New Yorker," I said to the driver of my Checker, "by the way he refuses to call Sixth the Avenue of the Americas." By rough count it was the four hundredth time I had made that observation. Once in the city, I could not stop beginning to work. Why was that white-sneakered citizen of Spanish descent reading Forbes in front of the Art Students League? Wrong tune. A moving van parked alongside Bendel's in broad daylight? Surefire hanky-panky. There in front of À La Vieille Russie was Arthur ("French Fries") Walker, whom I had the honor of busting for pimping too conspicuously in the lobby of the Pierre. Oh, the book I had on that dude. His love for middle-aged Jewish women (eventually his undoing). His brief stint as one of the Low-Balls in downtown Philly. (He did the falsetto parts.) But why go on? We turned up Madison. Could that possibly be a zee of "girl" going down in the window table of the Carlton Delicatessen? A certified class collar for your correspondent (not to speak of the publicity splash for proprietors David and Aaron). I pushed on. Had it been a key, I might have asked Purification Riviero to jam on the brakes. But for a trifling zee? *C'était sans importance.* We moved further east, locus point of the cinephiles, me making a mental note to see the latest by Paul Mazursky, that Flaubert of the Polo Lounge.

I scooped up my mail (mostly Carte Blanche brochures, tempting me with Founding Father coin collections), noted that Upper Class Productions was still in business on the floor above me (four hard-working light hooks, masquerading as P.R. consultants—and they had better hurry up and send the red-headed NYU sophomore down for tea and whatever or that would be the end of their neighbor-detective's live-and-let-live policy).

I took down my "Beware, Scarlet Fever Victim" door sign (with Spanish translation) and went straight to the plants, which I was happy to see were hanging on gamely. I turned off WRVR and thought for a moment of all the wasted Paul Desmond and John Coltrane (designed to fake out pillagers and looters) that had poured out into an empty room. What happened to all that music, where did it go and what a nifty riddle to pose to my Civilization and Philosophy Seminar at Hunter on Thursday night (paid for by Mayor Beame and all you nice taxpayers out there).

Everything was as I had left it; my framed Police Academy diploma, machete collection, indirectly lighted train set, freezerful of Frankie and Johnnie steaks, which the boys were kind enough to send over as a door prize for the Homicide Cruise (canceled due to budget-cutting). Gently cursing myself for forgetting to pick up fresh garlic at Gristede's, I commenced to whip up a Caesar salad. And then I noticed that my Clue Box was missing.

That made three. The demise of Crystal; her taping of my voice (and it better not be the conversation I thought it was); and now my vanished Clue Box. Admittedly, there was little of value in the leather portmanteau, a gift from a Lindsay aide for successfully guarding his body aboard an El Al airliner en route to a fact-finding tour of Haifa (his goal: to find out how that wicked city kept its fleshpots under control). As I recall, there was a finger (in alcohol) for study in relation to my dildo beef; a swatch of a Chilean diplomat's sports jacket, to be boiled down into what might or might not turn out to be liquid coke; a can opener with an almost microscopic speck of either blood or Tabasco sauce, related to an unclosed squawk in Harlem; a copy of

*The Sayings of Marcus Aurelius,* signed "To Herb Barker, My Favorite Crime Buster" by Mario Puzo at Patsy's. (He did not have a spare copy of *The Fortunate Pilgrim.*)

You get the idea. Couple of fortune cookies, an old address book with RAQUEL WELCH'S PHONE NUMBER in it from when I once almost got eleven weeks' Technical Adviser work on one of her pictures except that (story of my life) the budget couldn't sweat it. So there was nothing, really, that I could not get through the day without. It wasn't as if Urban Renewal or the future of Southeast Asia was at stake. I just wanted my Clue Box back. And it meant somebody had been lurking in my apartment, which gave me, allegedly hard-boiled soul that I am, a queasy feeling. Sudden unexplained noises give me the willies, too. I have to see what I am dealing with, and even then, I am not always such a complete bargain—as evidenced by my throat bite.

I summoned Conchita, who worked six days a week for the light hooks upstairs and one afternoon a week for me. Conchita had the only living duplicate of my key and was as honest as the day is long, which fact was helped along by my knowing about her husband, Carmen, and the three-to-seven he had staring him in the face if anyone ever looked into the hot-car complaint that was out on him in Rhode Island. Which I would never consider doing. Using signs and giggles, Conchita indicated that a man, "very nice," had appeared in the hallway and helped her rewire the vacuum cleaner so she could make my carpeting "very nice." I now had two very nices to work with, so with a light *droite du seigneur* tap on her charming Latin *tochis,* I dismissed Conchita, since I did not want to find myself drowning in a sea of evidence.

What happens with one of these Gucci-style slayings is that a couple of hundred East Side sleuths are turned loose and get to trip over each other's toes for forty-eight hours. If no suspect is popped within the appointed time, the team quickly gets trimmed back to two or three sluggish, heavy-lidded types and anyone in the Bureau with some kind of an erection to see justice served, which in this case, of course, was me. I dropped around the Bureau a day early to get congratulated on my suntan. In the lobby, dealers of a small-fry variety rushed forward to show me how clean their arms were, a salute to my two exciting years as a rookie junk dick. This display of clean arms was a sure sign that my old friends would be back at the Maritime Union before the morrow, making quick buys from Norwegian seamen, a few of whom would turn out to be (heh, heh) members of our team. Twenty-four hours had passed and all Gumm had so far was an Israeli who claimed he was a highly feared Secret Service operative and a Tel Aviv literary agent. He was a Jack La Lanne's regular, had no alibi and was on record as once having picked up Crystal at J.F.K. in the rain and taken her for drinks at the University Club. Gumm thought he had something and I thought he didn't. "When you take this Jewish guy and put him together with the fact that the blood drops point right to the sauna...." *Avec le minimum de politesse,* I told Gumm I would catch his act some other time.

I went to the Property Clerk's office and listened to the tape and of course, it was exactly the one I was hoping it wouldn't be: A six-in-the-morning call I had made to Crystal on the occasion of my fortieth birthday which was supposed to go by smoothly and didn't. I'll just hum a few bars. It had the word *vulnerable* in there six times; followed closely by three or four "afraids." Knowing my six-in-the-morning style, it's a safe guess I used the phrase "inability to form a close relationship" a few times—I didn't listen to the whole thing. This is what she had to go and tape. I am seriously not allowed to drink and I had excused myself on my birthday, operating on the thesis that who tapes such things? Crystal does, or did, anyway. Under the circumstances, it was going to be difficult to ask her why. I just hoped she hadn't made a deal with Carly Simon to bring out a whole album of the stuff.

What I had to do was tap-dance around for another twenty-four hours; there was no rule that said it couldn't be creative tap-dancing. These are some of the things I did:

1) Went to the police equipment store and got a little more lead stuck in my slapjack (basically a time-killer).
2) Visited New Jersey. The girl, not the state. New Jersey Ryan. Friend of Crystal's until they had a falling-out over some insoluble issue. A disputed tube of eyeliner. Something along those lines. New Jersey is an M.A.W. (model-actress-whatever, with an emphasis on the whatever); strong evidence exists that it was her name that kept her from making That Extra Step. Georgia, fine; Carolina, no problem; Mexico, why not? Even Israel gets an outside chance. New Jersey? No way. But she stubbornly clung to it—need I say that there are people like that?—and now she is a soft thirty-eight or so and it's a bit academic. Dates South Americans, wearily turns up at discotheque openings, and will act in porno films if someone uses the word *art* with some regularity, pays her slightly above Equity minimum, and lets her wear a thin mask (the last is negotiable). Total earthly possessions if she were knocked off à la Crystal: a trunkload of junk jewelry, second-time-around Givenchy gowns and (surprise!) an authentic Klee, which she hides in her makeup table. She told me I never quite realized how hard Crystal took it when we split up. I said I understood and she said, "No, you don't understand. She really, really took it hard." I said I *knew* she took it hard and she shrugged and said, "You don't understand." Then, finally, I understood.
3) Got a haircut from the Turk, who told me there was a new

kind of wise guy in town, blond-macho-gay, stalked the new discos, got off on sudden, unprovoked openings of people's heads in men's rooms. The Turk gave you very little, including the work he did on your sideburns, but what he gave you was choice.

4) Visited New Jersey, the state this time, not the girl. Went to see Ronnie Steamroom (I don't know his real name—Lieberson, I think), who runs half a dozen health clubs in that state after having been encouraged to leave Manhattan by some serious gentlemen he had rudely misled in a bat-guano commodities deal. And if he ever came back across the George Washington Bridge, even to get his dry cleaning, he was a strong favorite to show up as a McDonaldburger. He told me that it was not uncustomary for parties to go on in health clubs, late at night, when the last ad exec had left and the sauna was cold. This was not much, but it was something.

5) Dropped by to see Katrina, my streamlined mid-seventies securities analyst grown-up Danish girl friend. Had our basic dispute over who had picked up whom that first time. I let her win that one. Had our usual debate over who it was that was horny on this particular occasion. I gave her that one, too. Disrobed and went into a brief squabble, in mime this time, over who it was that was going to put it to whom and who was going to do the putting. I handed that one over, giving her three for three. Anyone who knocks this new woman's thing has been hanging around with the wrong people.

These are some of the colorful results of my activities: New Jersey's Klee got slashed, hateful thing to see and don't even bother asking if it was insured; as he got off the E train at Sutphin Boulevard, someone threw hair dye in the Turk's eyes (he's all right); an unknown party got into Katrina's apartment—we fixed the time at 4:15 in the A.M.—and broke one of her kneecaps with a standard Philadelphia-style crowd-control hickory night stick—left at the foot of the bed. Nothing appeared to have happened to Ronnie Steamroom. Thunderously obvious conclusion:

Whatever it was I was doing, a person or persons unknown had found it unattractive.

For my part, I hated the kneecap thing. There just wasn't any way to be wry or ironical about it. Because of the nervousness of some of her securities deals, I had gotten Katrina a permit for a thirty-eight which she kept in her night table—but there had not been any way for her to get at it. The party had made his or her entrance and exit via some jalousied windows, which was no mean feat, since Katrina's apartment was kind of a rooftop eyrie in an old leftover super-tall brownstone in the East Seventies. An agile person, to put it mildly, had pulled this thing off. Whoever tore up the Klee had had to do some fancy foot-work, too, come to think of it, since New Jersey, at the moment, had been living in a woman's residence with a dead elevator. More intricate rooftop action here. I stayed with Katrina for twenty-four hours at Flower Hospital and for twenty-four hours I was in love with her. It takes some-thing along those lines to get me to go that way—a busted kneecap.

The following day, I asked Gumm to assign me officially to the Crystal case. He said I ought to finish up the dildo item first and I maintained that I could handle them both at the same time. He said I knew perfectly well I could not handle two things at once and I said I know, I know, but that I had thought it through and was convinced I could do the two of them. "With this Crystal girl," he said "...you weren't by any chance...uh...?"

"Wiggling it in there? Is that what you were going to ask?"

"Well, actually..."

"Because if that's what you were going to ask, I suggest you don't ask it."

"Why don't you just go to work?"

"Why don't I?"

And I did. But we had measured each other for a beat or two and it was Gumm who had decided to break it off and I have a sneaking suspicion it was because of my throat bite.

It had been a humiliating experience. I owed one to someone. You would be amazed at all the times that tension causes us fellows in crime to go at each other, with serious consequences. It certainly would be a source of great embarrassment to all parties concerned if I were to take my feelings out on old Gumm, my immediate superior.

I realized it wasn't *Swann's Way,* but somehow had the feeling I would be able to read the Medical Examiner's report on Crystal with objectivity. So I curled up with a copy in the Property Office and whipped right through "Liver Weight and Condition" and "Contents of Intestine." "Quality of Urine" gave me no trouble at all; indeed, I read it with mounting fascination. It was not until I came to "Quantity of Semen, and Location of Tears in Vaginal Membrane" that I felt a need to set the manuscipt aside. The prose rhythms were sound, the imagery vivid, but it just wasn't for me. Latent Prints had come up with a few smudges on the parallel bars that were traced to an agent in the William Morris office (on the day of the slaying he was in Massachusetts catching Dick Shawn in *Richard III*). Gumm's Israeli suspect had knocked over the polygraph test as if it were a Syrian lemonade stand. I could not quite pinpoint the quarter we were in, but I had the feeling it was late and we were down three touchdowns.

With no particular song in my heart, I went over to check out the Health Spa. I told the receptionist—Italian, mischievous—she oughta be in pictures and she told me if I didn't take a special two-month tummy-trim program, I might not make it through the summer. I told her she had it all wrong, that the roll above my belt was a deliberate attempt to cultivate a kind of soft, casual, diplomatic Kissinger Look. Then I showed her my tin and the romance came to an abrupt ending. I looked over Crystal's lockers and I got very glum. A sign had been pasted across them: "Not in Use." What was it, some kind of mourning period? For the lockers? I didn't see much exercise being perpetrated, but there was a lot of arguing going on. Maybe that's the way they reduced. They argued it off. A fellow said he heard the Ali-Foreman fight was fixed and now he could not enjoy it anymore.

"But you *did* enjoy it," said the guy next to him.

"I *did*," said the first fellow, "but I don't anymore."

"You can't suddenly not enjoy something you once enjoyed," his friend argued (with some logic, I thought).

"The hell I can't!"

I had some figures jiggling around in my head...arrival of duty detective, probable time of death, onset of rigor ...but they were not going to do me much good. I am bad on time and terrific on shoe imprints. No one else in the Bureau puts much stock in them, and as a result I am looked upon as kind of a lacrosse player. On President Street. It was an off-hour. On hand were a couple of self-employed decorators and a few Depression Victim execs working out to make sure they looked under forty. I covered the gym carpeting; the only one to give me any grief was an actor I recognized as playing cop parts in all the movies shot in New York. He wanted to know what I was doing on the gym floor, fully dressed. It was enough to make a fellow go for his weapon.

In fifteen minutes I established firmly what I sort of knew before. That someone incredibly agile was in the picture.

I went over to Melon's and ordered three bacon cheeseburgers, each one a classic. Jack O'Neill wanted to know if I had come off a fast.

"No, I been looking at a lot of exercise machines."

Then I headed for the Donnell division of the Public Library, where I do my thinking. Much thinking transpires there, and the sound of all that thinking helps my thinking. I checked out *Jewish American Literature: An Anthology* and spread it in front of me to make me look honest. The first thing I thought was that it's true what they say about homicide. But then, I could not remember what it was that they said. That third cheeseburger had cost me a step. Then I remembered: With a homicide, you had to be there. That is, there was no way to compensate for the fact that I was not on the set when the body was discovered. You could look at M.E. reports until the cows came home, but there was no way to duplicate the feel and tone and impact of that moment when the lockers got opened. It's like trying to describe to someone how good *The Sorrow and the Pity* is.

So I had to take another tack; forgive the clumsy syntax, but if I didn't know about Crystal, who in the goddamned hell else did? (Hardly realizing it, I had read a little Wallace Markfield and enjoyed the hell out of him. I made a note to pick up *Teitlebaum's Window.*) Then I forced myself to focus on my affair with Crystal and for some reason I could not get off the Cranky Period. *You don't really love me. You don't understand me. You don't understand how a woman feels. You're selfish.* Hardly Simone de Beauvoir–level insights, but she certainly did have a good fix on me. *Michael was the only one. He understood me. Only Michael.* And that's the name, of course, that I was searching for. Crystal had made more than a few stops en route to my particular hot-dog stand (as she was to make others after she checked out). But she had tarried for quite some time at Michael's place. Her other lovers had been cruel, each affair ending, if memory served, with Crystal's being shoved down a flight of stairs. Michael was different, however. He had never

shoved her down a flight of stairs. And once she had decided to push on, he had never recovered. He tried other
women, Crystal lookalikes, but that didn't work out. He
lived alone, modestly, upstate, where they had lived together. According to Crystal, he kept candles in the window. A rich kid, he had had to keep a low profile because
of something involving an inheritance. I was never jealous
of Michael. Crystal had shown me his photograph, lots of
hair, Grand Prix–type face. No problem. I liked the fact
that he had once been good to her and thought that was
very middle-aged Continental of me.

The department had interviewed everyone in the city of
New York, including the fast-growing Dominican popu-
lation, but I had a feeling they had missed Michael. It
meant I would have to give up a Kurosawa Festival, but
now I knew what I was doing the next morning.

I headed back to my place; more nonsense of a particularly odious type. Someone had been poking around a
second time. The lock was good—I used something that
had been sold as "Beyond Even Medeco"—but the windows had been fiddled with. My vertical-screen Sony (which,
frankly, had come off a truck) was intact. Same for my
harman/kardon stereo (also off a truck, except I pitched
in and bought the speakers). But someone had been fooling around in my bed. There was much blanket-and-sheet
turmoil and in the middle of this petit whirlwind of bac-
chanalia lay the missing finger from my Clue Box. Sans
alcohol. I took it all like a soldier until I realized some son
of a bitch had grabbed my train set.

Up I went, one flight, to the hookers, High Class Unlimited, or whatever the hell they called themselves. I talked
to the woman in charge of the equipment box, whips, leg
shackles, etc., and asked if she had heard anything funny
transpiring in my apartment. I also pointed out that I

wanted the red-headed NYU sophomore right that second
or a moving van there Monday, since I was tired of hearing
bond salesmen being whipped at five in the morning. She
said she hadn't heard anything funny in my apartment
and that the redhead only did "quickies." I said get her
out of there fast and she could string together a number
of "quickies" and it would do nicely. The redhead was a
gentle girl and seemed to feel a heavy sense of responsi-
bility about her assignment, that is, the keeping open of
High Class Unlimited. "I think I've forgotten something,"
she kept saying, as we went about our nefarious work. "Are
there some things I'm leaving out?" I told her she was
doing fine. Later (as they used to say before the Erotic
Revolution) we sat around and discussed art history, which
she was studying at NYU before embarking on a marital
venture. She was a nice person. She just wasn't my train
set.

It is said around the Police Academy and such that cops
of all races, religions, creeds and geographies speak with
a single tongue and are united in a tight coppish broth-
erhood. That is probably true, the sole exception being
the New York City detective, who is viewed in the outlying
districts as some kind of Armenian type. Such was the
nature of my reception when I made a courtesy stop at the
Piedmont Police Station and inquired as to the where-
abouts of Michael Jeffrey, Crystal's former lover that
everybody forgot about, including me. Coolness and brisk-
ness were the order of the day. Prodding about for their
soft underbelly, I complimented them on their Emergency
Service and Ballistics Unit, which I had heard was the equal
of any in the country, including Chicago and especially
New York.
A breakthrough occurred and I even got a couple of fat
beaming smiles. Michael Jeffrey had died in a fire about

a year back. The fire was a little "funny"—enough so to justify a coroner's inquest, which had come up empty. He had lived with a woman of international extraction who had hauled ass about twenty minutes after the inquest report. This meant that all the time Crystal was telling me about Michael pining away, there was no Michael. Indeed, Michael, long ago, had gone up in smoke. Which meant that maybe Crystal had never seen Guam, Rio and that cooking school in Brest, either. Was it going to turn out that she was a girl from Bayside? Or that I had imagined her, the way I'm still not absolutely sure I once took a sudden impulsive trip to Trondheim? Very Transcendental Meditative and very unsettling. Michael's parents still lived in Piedmont, and it was to their house that I hied.

My guess was that they were Jewish folks who had gone over to the other team of which there is no one in the world more bland and Apple Pie than such ex-Semites. Mr. Jeffrey (né Jefkowitz?) showed me football trophies, and the like, involving his son, Michael. Such people do not cry or show grief after a loss. They show trophies. There was also a sister, Dolly Jeffrey, who was evidently made of more ethnic stuff and had never bought the inquest report on her brother for a second. Several weeks back, she had headed for New York City, who knows, maybe to nose around and do something about it.

They say a man's job is where he lands; a fellow gets into the shingle business, not because he has always dreamed of shingles, but because he happens to fall into it. There's him, there's shingles and he goes and does them. I don't happen to subscribe to this theory. My feeling is that he and shingles have always had a rendezvous with destiny. Something drew him to shingles. And thus it is with homicide. It is no accident that I am a homicider, and the way I know this is when I hear something like Dolly Jeffrey's heading, two weeks ago, for New York to check further into her brother's death. My heart begins to thump like a son of a bitch. There is no difference from when it pounded the first time on the one I cracked in the Holland Tunnel (see *Daily News,* April 9, 1955, page 5, my first collar). My heart behaved that way on my premiere collar, and it will on my last. I'm not talking about the collar so much as when I can smell the collar.

Shift now to Dr. Wen, the Taiwan Tooth Fairy, Cavity Man to the Stars, whose I.D. on Crystal's mouth I hadn't been too pleased with, right from the gitgo. In one sense, it was better than fingerprints, which have been known to wear off in some cases (age, disease); no two mouths are ever alike. On the other hand, who in the hell was there to challenge him? He had done some work on my bite (I was a Crystal referral), quitting in mid-mouth, as it were, when he spotted a flaw in my Detective's Dental Insurance Plan. Then and there, he had lost my vote as Mr. Integrity. I recalled he had done some work for the navy in World War II. I had a marker out with Naval Intelligence which I decided to call in; within six hours I learned that his tie with the navy had been canceled when they discovered he had been making deals with naval pilots to falsify their dental reports—and thereby get them grounded. How the evil spool did unwind on our Oriental friend. With two of my colleagues, I lit out for Versailles, or its equivalent thereof, which Dr. Wen had built for himself in Great Neck Estates. A male servant, of prune-like disposition, informed us that Dr. Wen could not be disturbed at the moment, as he was occupied discussing root-canal work with one of Alan King's nephews. Though my pulse quickened at the mention of the famed Great Neck comedian, I insisted that my business could not hold, and proceeded, along with my fellows, to the main hall.

Maps spread out before him, Dr. Wen appeared to be

planning bike trips through Vancouver. No nephew of the
celebrated Great Neck jester was in evidence. After first
tossing up a great cloud of Eastern civility, Dr. Wen managed to get across his point that we were motherfouquers
for invading his home. I told him I knew about his naval
caper. Nothing. I introduced Karl Polski of Immigration
and Customs, who produced documents indicating that
Dr. Wen was an illegal alien, even though the fix had been
put in several years back, the point being that a new administration was in that didn't know or care about the fix.
We got him a little on that one. For my concluding act, I
brought on, to a tidy round of applause, Arnie Dix, who
had taken over for me in Junk and had chapter and verse
on Dr. Wen's Xylocaine gig and how part of his allotment
found its way to inmates at Attica at a net gain to the doctor
of some fifteen large a year. What I am saying is that we
had the middle clogged, the wide lanes blocked, and Dr.
Wen had no outside shot. He told me he had falsified the
dental I.D.

Meaning the girl in the lockers was not Crystal. Meaning
nine chances out of ten that the girl was Dolly Jeffrey, who
had investigated her brother's death only too well. Meaning ten chances out of ten that it was Crystal, alive, well,
bright-eyed and bushy-tailed, who had gotten Dr. Wen to
falsify the I.D.

All of the above suggestions checked out.

"How in the hell did she get you to do a thing like that?"
I asked this question of the not so good Dr. Wen, after I
had made a quick call to Gumm and brought the fellow
up to date. And no sooner had I asked than I knew *la
réponse*. The same way she had gotten me to shake a gynecologist down for her couch. Or that, for no apparent
reason, a leading Wasp financier had handed her a ten
percent interest in a chain of Greek luncheonettes. And
that an East Sixty-seventh Street landlord had rented her

the reception hall of a former emerging-nation embassy for one hundred and sixty dollars a month, utilities thrown in. It was all tied in to the trouble I used to have when people asked me, "Exactly what does she do?" I always sort of knew what she did, but I could never catch her doing it and I was smart enough not to try too hard. It just wasn't any fun knowing, finally, once and for all, that she did do it.

Now, apparently, she had a new hobby, depositing parts of young girls in lockers of health clubs. By no stretch of the imagination could I imagine Crystal actually taking apart such girls, but now I had to wonder about that, too. When I first began to half live with her, I remember the subject coming up of what she would do if she ever caught me in an extracurricular activity on her. "Twist your neck, break your bones, crack your feet, make them all into powder and throw them in the toilet." All of this accompanied by graceful, almost Noh Theater gestures. Charming, I had thought to myself. Absolutely charming. Real storybook stuff, throwing witches into fires, slicing off the dragon's head. "You got to hear this," I told a group of my friends. "It's the most goddamned charming thing you ever heard." And I would have her say it for a couple of friends, who agreed it was charming, too, maybe not as charming as I thought it was, but, no question, heavy in the charm department.

Now I had to wonder. I thought of New Jersey's words (probably the only time anyone had ever thought of her words): "*You'll never quite understand how hard she took it when you two split up.*" And then I made myself stop wondering. There was no way Crystal herself could have actually performed the taking apart of another pretty human being. Maybe the packing and loading, but never the other. And that was that.

But she was on *some* kind of campaign.

Taking back my trains, for example, unmistakably had her touch. Stealing my Clue Box? A Crystal special. Klee-slashing, a definite maybe and using my bed for mad venereous bouts, right on the beam, although I am not so sure where the finger fit in (and would prefer not to think about it). The dye in the Turk's eyes?—I don't think so; smashing Katrina's kneecap, not her style. Proceeding along these lines, how would she be able to swing into people's windows at nosebleed altitudes, given as she was to walking into buildings and falling off ladders due to false pride and an unwillingness to get involved with contact lenses, even though I told her how good the soft ones were?

Let me avail myself of an opportunity to set things down the way my Hunter College professor of rhetoric would like it. (The reader will be kind enough to sprinkle in ibid.s and *loc. cit.*s, since we have not gotten to them and won't until the stretch drive of the fall semester.)

1.) Crystal was mad at me.
2.) She did not want anyone getting close to the fire, the fire that Michael Jeffrey was suspiciously caught in, that is.
3.) Crystal was very mad at me.
4.) She had acquired a new and reckless partner on her ride along Life's Highway.

It was this last item that had me stuck on a dime when I received one of those lovely bonuses that occasionally accrue to us lonely souls who toil in the homicidal vineyard. My bench came to the rescue, pouring in a badly needed bucket. Gumm called. At God-alone-knows-what punishing cost to the taxpayer, his men had established that Crystal had taken up with a limo driver. (In her heyday, Crystal would hire limos to pick up *Women's Wear Daily*.) He had been a stunt man for Linguini Westerns (budgeted slightly higher than Spaghetti Westerns). His nickname was "Loose." There was a sheet on him, peppered with assault and battery notations. He was no stranger to the slam. His style was to open the heads—suddenly and unprovoked— of the following types in discotheque men's rooms:

a.) Anyone who ignored him.
b.) Anyone who paid attention to him.
c.) Anyone who did none of the above.

This petty quirk had made it difficult for him to secure employment in his chosen occupation and driven him into the limo-driving game. A note on his sheet used the phrase "Blond; macho-gay." A further notation indicated that— by way of introducing himself—he was known to tumble down three or four flights of stairs. The Turk, of course, had alerted me to the presence of such a person in the neighborhood watering spots. And had gotten dye in his eyes for his trouble.

From all evidence, Crystal and her new partner (how it pains me to use that godforsaken nickname—all right, here goes), "Loose," were still in the area, seemingly unaware that I knew she wasn't the locker girl. As attested to by the fact that Ronnie Steamroom was pistol-whipped on Mulberry Street while making a surreptitious trip to the city for some special Italian salad oils.

Though points would be awarded for speed at this juncture, I had now to contend with yet another phenomenon that will be recognizable to those who at one time or another have engaged in police activities. It is called Fear of the Collar. What happens is that just when you are on the edge of wrapping up a case, there comes about a sudden and obviously self-defeating urge to see a Clint Eastwood film, study macramé, attend the Stuttgart Ballet, fix defective wall switches and perhaps enter into heated debates on whether a Ducati can stay with and even burn a Kawasaki at one hundred and twenty miles an hour (entering Hartford). The phenomenon was once explained to me by a departmental psychologist (yet another budget victim, long gone, forced to go into film criticism) as having to do with not wanting to outdistance your dad. In the oedipal race for your mom. Or something like that. (I once had it down cold.) If one's dad was a cop, F.O.T.C. became all the more fierce. So I had to fight it like a sumbitch. And fight it I did, walking out on Eastwood's *Eiger Sanction* when he was halfway up the mountain. (Forgive me, Clint, although frankly, the second I saw you show up as an art history professor in the first frame I sensed you were in big trouble.)

My throat bite began to ache. Was there such a thing as arthritis of the throat, responsive to tension and seasonal changes?

In our heyday, or hey-season, Crystal, though almost fully grown, had been a great hide-and-seek player. Few people had time to conceal themselves in closets, under beds, behind hatracks and then leap out on a person's shoulders, but Crystal did. The problem was where in the city of New York to look for a once-charming but increasingly violent hide-and-seek player and her limo-driving stuntman friend? I had two thoughts: We had once vowed to further cement our romance with the acquisition of a Rhodesian Ridgeback, a new breed of dog known not so much for its white-supremacist attitudes as its willingness to learn a trick a day. There was a kennel in Brooklyn. Crystal and her companion were holed up in it, the stunt man keeping his artillery focused on the street, Crystal playing with the Ridgeback puppies. Dreadful idea, right? *D'accord.* Another Brooklyn idea was the trailer-court man who was an expert in hallucinogenic mushrooms—grew them, ate them, shared them with interested friends. Crystal had been fascinated by the fellow, had popped a few and stared at the moonlight over Sheepshead Bay while I waited in the squad. That's another place I might have a peek at.

Except that while I was having these thoughts, I was also feeling my way along some rope of instinct that led me to the IRT, en route to the South Bronx. Where I had grown up and been raised by Helen Reilly, who for all practical purposes was my mother, my own folks having gone off a cliff when I was a babe—a whole separate story. How did Helen's death affect me? Let's just say that I couldn't even look at the South Bronx on a map. Any case that took me there got transferred over to some close colleague. With a gun to my head, I could not think of Helen Reilly's old phone number (and mine), much less dial it. When she died I told Heavy Eddie, the handyman, just to get rid of everything in the apartment, and not tell me what he'd done with it. I buried her and then I blanked out the whole thing. And now I was taking a casual subway ride to the South Bronx. They sure had a lot of blind ads in the subway. Appeals for blind vets, blind moms, blind dogs. Anything blind went right up there in the Bronx subway ads. To give you an idea of my feelings about going up to the South Bronx—looking at all that blind material was comic relief. A sneak preview of Tati's latest.

I had told Crystal all about Helen Reilly. "I wish you could've known her," I'd say.

"I do know her," she would say back to me.

Some vegetable guy would try to sell us defective tomatoes and Crystal would say, "Helen Reilly would have told him to shove those tomatoes up his ass." And she was always right. Not on the precise language—Helen Reilly was a lot softer than Crystal imagined her—but on the sense of her; she really knew what Helen Reilly would have thought or said. Very eerie stuff. If the faithful reader will permit one last saccharine note, Crystal was probably the only one in the world who knew what Helen Reilly meant to me. Which is why I was taking this jaunt to the South Bronx. Which is not exactly St. Tropez. To add to the merriment, I was soaking wet in a madras shirt and slacks. Which came from Barney's and not off a truck this time.

Getting off at Jerome Avenue and One Hundred Sixty-first Street was easy. Strolling over to the old apartment on Morris Avenue would be the hard part. Climbing the stairs and ringing the doorbell? Like being told you have a touch of the Big C. I found some childhood rocks I used to jump down from in Joyce Kilmer Park, and as a charming diversion, totally fruitless, as it turned out, jumped down from them again. I looked at Yankee Stadium and thought of Charley Keller showing up for a game, dark face, brooding shoulders. That helped me about as much as a children's aspirin. I crossed the Grand Concourse, thinking of the safety slogan with which I'd won a carton of Thanx candy bars: "Follow the red and green; you'll wind up in the pink." (So how come I'm not writing for Carson?) I was on Morris Avenue, a division of San Juan now, staring at the building, a sudden middle-aged vomiter. Heavy Eddie, big, black, the handyman from the birth of the building, around one hundred and five now, came out and by way of greeting me, hit me with his belly. Lot of haw haws, welcome back to the plantation, Massah Herbie, and you'll never guess who took over your mommy's apartment. Amazing. Took the furniture that I had stashed, the whole thing.

"I know, I know, I know," I said. "I know."

"Prettiest little girl, and she said she knew your mommy. Up there with a gentleman she says is her brother or something."

"I know, I know, I know."

Up to date, trendy as ever, Heavy Eddie wanted to swap Robin Yount ancedotes with me; I figured I might as well get right at it. You're scheduled for surgery, don't put it off. In the great tradition, I laid a dime on Eddie, got the key from him, took the deepest breath of my career, and walked up the stairs to 3N. Then I took the second deepest breath of my career and committed breaking and entering on my old apartment in the South Bronx.

The piano was in the wrong part of the living room, the beige rug was poorly placed, the imitation fireplace had real logs in front of it—but apart from a few blunders along these lines, everything was much the way I remembered it. This was a bit boring, since I had sensed I would find it this way. Nonboring came when I took a little stroll into the bedroom. I'm telling you, if ever there comes a time when there is no David Merrick, someone ought to get in touch with this girl. In my mother's bed, yet. With her friend. And in my mother's nightgown. Beat that, Mr. Krafft-Ebing.

"Hi, Herbie," said Crystal. "What do you think of what I did? This is Loose. Loose, Herbie."

Are you ready for the fact that I said, "How do you do?" And that we shook hands. We did.

Quickly, however, the temperature rose. Forget about the air conditioner. Forget the South Bronx. Think Gobi Desert. Loose was in a crouch, a mannerism left over from one of his Italian Westerns.

"I'm not gonna pull a knife on you," he said, his voice strangely high-pitched, Irish choirboy. True to his word, he did not. What he pulled was a broken bottle (Châteauneuf-du-Pape, I later learned) and with a deft and rather graceful underhanded movement (that showed a certain familiarity with Borges' early classic, *The South*) made contact with my shoulder, producing five small fountains of blood. I would like to be able to say that the dreamlike quality of the moment was numbing. It was not. It hurt like a son of a bitch.

"Oh, Loose," said Crystal, sitting up petulantly, my dead mother's nightgown drawn, with feigned casualness, to just the right level above her knees. She scolded him as if he had dropped ashes on the rug.

The time had come for me to unsheath my weapon, which I did, although—due to the highly personal nature of our trinella—there was little chance I would immediately go boom boom. Alert to my physical and psycho-schmycho discomfiture, Loose seized the opportunity to make tracks. I made them, too, following him through the door past the incinerator (what a proud day it was when we said hello to that class innovation and farewell to the hellish dumbwaiter) and to the end of the hallway. It was at this point that I got to see firsthand his famous calling card, falling down three flights of stairs...and not hurting himself. After a quick sniff of what I took to be ancient traces of delicious Bronx cooking smells, I followed him to the building lobby, across to the second, or "D," wing. Here, Loose treated me to a new wrinkle, what appeared to be his tumbling back *up* the stairs—a variation he may very well have introduced for my benefit. And then we were on the roof, but not before I had paused—amazingly—for a split second at 6F, home of Dick Schreiber, a plodder who had gone on to fame in Boston cardiology. If Schreiber, a grind, believe me (I'm not talking about Levinson of 4F, who really had some stuff), attained those heights, you mean to tell me I couldn't have made it in medicine, at least in anesthesiology?

To the roof. What followed would most likely have been your traditional cops-and-robbers chase across the roof-tops of the Bronx, with the possible result that Loose would have leaped and stumbled and twirled his way to freedom—since the only moving target I've ever hit was a skeet or two on the deck of an Oslo "party boat," another one of my great vacation ideas. And also, I get nauseated on rooftops. So Loose would probably be free and padding about in Venezuela today if he had not made the mistake of killing Heavy Eddie, the one-hundred-and-five-year-old handyman who had once rushed me to Morrisania Hospital when a collie bit my six-year-old *tochis*. He killed him with another of those goddamned broken bottles. I could not figure out where he was getting them until I realized he had one of those Gucci shoulder bags filled with them. He had some style. I don't know how Heavy Eddie got up there so fast. They had probably repaired the elevator, the first time it was running smoothly in twenty-two years. And he was up on the rooftop and when I passed him I knew he was dead because of his smile. I know that dead smile. There is a dead frown and a dead smile, but they are both dead. One thing I know is dead. So I forgot the fact that we were running along Bronx rooftops (well sort of, anyway) and I took off after Loose and held my own. That is, I kept the gap between us down to around half a rooftop. To give him his due, it was because he was stopping to do tricks along the way. What was he doing, auditioning? I would probably still be running after him out in Gila Bend somewhere if it hadn't been for the fact that he stopped for a minute and did some leg extensions. I don't know. Maybe he had a legitimate cramp. I could have let one fly right then and there and put an end to the shabby episode in that manner, except that I guess I had something else in mind all along. When we were at close quarters, he unsnapped the Gucci bag and pulled out another bottle which he broke on the base of a combination clothesline/TV antenna. I assumed this bottle had my name on it. I waited a couple of beats, faked once to my right—thought of Heavy Eddie, my mother, Crystal in my mother's god-

damned nightgown, the two of them in my mother's bed,
all this to kind of get myself morally covered—and then
I bit his throat out.

   As I've probably indicated, I had wanted to make that
move for some time and had been looking for the right
opportunity. What had happened is that when I incurred
my own throat bite (on Broadway, right across from Za-
bar's) I had double-pumped, in the classic Walt Frazier
style, and the wino I was trying to belt out had not gone
for it. He had not, of course, bitten my throat entirely out,
but he had gotten his teeth in there pretty good, enough
to make me sleepy every morning of my life. And after a
good sleep. So I guess it had been simmering away, sub-
liminally, for some time. And, of course, I also had Dr.
Wen's bite to work with, so I suppose, unconsciously, I had
wanted to get my money's worth, too. So I had done it
back to Loose. Not double-pumping, and with only a single
head fake. Which he had gone for. Like so many of these
things, once you get it done it really isn't all that much.
Let me share with you something that I have learned. The
fantasy of biting out an entire throat is much more stim-
ulating than the actual deed.
   It did not look as if much of a crowd was going to collect
on the rooftop. It did not look as if anyone had been up
there since F.D.R. died. So I figured I had time for a
cigarillo or two.
   I went back down to my old apartment and used the
phone.
   "Who are you calling, Herbie?" asked Crystal.
   "My answering service."
   She was tidying up, as if she were expecting six for dinner.
I sat down on my mother's old flowered living-room couch.
   "How do you like the way I fixed it up?" Crystal asked.
   "Great."

And it *was* great. Apart from a handbook on backgam-
mon hustling, a little out of sync, I could not see one goddamned item that was different from when I was growing
up and going to Cardinal Hayes. Just for fun, I checked
inside an Oriental vase on the bookshelves, and there were
the ten silver dollars Ned Reilly, my uncle, had given me
out of his Firemen's Pension Plan.

"What other girl would have done this for you?" she
asked.

"I sure as hell can't think of any."

The outrageous part is that if you stripped away a
few considerations—murder, throat-biting, masterpiece-
slashing, etc.—it *was* an extraordinary thing to do for a
fellow.

"Now, Herbie," she said. "What would you like to eat?"

"Anything," I said. "I'm not really that hungry."

"You say that all the time." She was an extraordinary
cook, and it was true, I did say it all the time and whatever
she came up with, I got rid of it like it was going out of
style and just about fainted with delight.

She brought out some cold tortellini, kind of half Italian,
half Jewish, and don't ask me how she pulled it off, but it
smelled a little Irish, too. I didn't actually get to taste it. I
think she was genuinely hurt and surprised when Gumm
and company showed up; I've never seen anyone look so
disdainful and aristocratic when they were getting the cuffs
put on them. Maybe Jackie O. would do it that way, but
she's the only one I can think of. I wasn't sure what I
wanted to do with the second chapter of my life, but two
things I definitely wanted to avoid were 1) watching Crystal
get hauled away in the paddy wagon and 2) meeting her
eyes.

I stayed around for half an hour or so, and actually
considered moving back to the old apartment. And then
I quickly unconsidered it. I locked it up; that night, I called

my brother in Laramie and told him to get rid of the place and its contents once and for all, take care of the whole thing. He's good at that stuff, even from Laramie.

No more surprises. (Just one, actually.) All that swinging in through windows had been Loose's work. The Piedmont crime-busters reopened the Michael Jeffrey arson case and it's pending. Crystal is in the women's slam, which I don't want to know about. Loose did the kneecap number. And they had dispatched Dolly Jeffrey as a team. (Loose had been dating a La Lanne's instructor, male gender—and had thusly gained access to the gym for the after-hours session.)

What continued to plague me was who it was that had actually done the Thanksgiving turkey slicing on Dolly Jeffrey. I had just about given Crystal a full pardon on that score when the tortellini I'd wisely refrained from eating came back from Microanalysis with a lab report setting forth a complete list of its unhappy ingredients ...flour, sugar, cornstarch, etc., that stuff, but also (for a quick death) potassium cyanide; (for a slow one) arsenic; and (presumably for a fascinating "fun" send-off) a certain species of Canarsie Trailer-Court Mushroom. All I could think of was: *That little rascal.*

And she *was* from Bayside.

—1975.

# Let's Hear It for a Beautiful Guy

*Sammy Davis is trying to get
a few months off for a complete
rest.—Earl Wilson, February 7, 1974.*

I HAVE BEEN TRYING TO GET a few months off for a complete rest, too, but I think it's more important that Sammy Davis get one. I feel that I can scrape along and manage somehow, but Sammy Davis always looks so strained and tired. The pressure on the guy must be enormous. It must have been a terrific blow to him when he switched his allegiance to Agnew and Nixon, only to have the whole thing blow up in his face. I was angry at him, incidentally, along with a lot of other fans of his, all of us feeling he had sold us down the river. But after I had thought it over and let my temper cool a bit, I changed my mind and actually found myself standing up for him, saying I would bet anything that Agnew and Nixon had made some secret promises to Sammy about easing the situation of blacks—ones that the public still doesn't know about. Otherwise, there was no way he would have thrown in his lot with that crowd. In any case, I would forgive the guy just about anything. How can I feel any other way when I think of the pleasure he's given me over the years, dancing and clowning around and wrenching those songs out of that wiry little body? Always giving his all, no matter what the composition of the audience. Those years of struggle with the Will Mastin Trio, and then finally making it, only to find marital strife staring him in the face. None of us will ever be able to calculate what it took out of him each time he had a falling-out with Frank. Is there any doubt who Dean and Joey sided with on those occasions? You can be sure Peter Lawford didn't run over to offer Sammy any solace. And does anyone ever stop to consider the spiritual torment he must have suffered when he made the switch to Judaism? I don't even want to talk about the eye. So, if anyone in the world does, he certainly deserves a few months off for a complete rest.

Somehow, I have the feeling that if I met Sammy, I could break through his agents and that entourage of his and convince him he ought to take off with me and get the complete rest he deserves. I don't want any ten percent, I don't want any glory; I just feel I owe it to him. Sure he's got commitments, but once and for all he's got to stop and consider that it's one time around, and no one can keep up that pace of his forever.

The first thing I would do is get him out of Vegas. There is absolutely no way he can get a few months' rest in that sanatorium. I would get him away from Vegas, and I would certainly steer clear of Palm Springs. Imagine him riding down Bob Hope Drive and checking into a hotel in the Springs! For a rest? The second he walked into the lobby, it would all start. The chambermaids would ask him to do a chorus of "What Kind of Fool Am I," right in the lobby, and, knowing Sammy and his big heart, he would probably oblige. I think I would take him to my place in New York, a studio. We would have to eat in, because if I ever showed up with Sammy Davis at the Carlton Delicatessen, where I have my breakfast, the roof would fall in. The owner would ask him for an autographed picture to hang up next to Dustin Hoffman's, and those rich young East Side girls would go to town on him. If they ever saw me walk in with Sammy Davis, that would be the end of his complete rest. They would attack him like vultures, and Sammy would be hard put to turn his back on them, because they're not broads.

We would probably wind up ordering some delicatessen from the Stage, although I'm not so sure that's a good idea; the delivery boy would recognize him, and the next thing you know, Sammy would give him a C note, and word would get back to Alan King that Sammy had ducked into town. How would it look if he didn't drop over to the Stage and show himself? Next thing you know, the news would reach Jilly's, and if Frank was in town—well, you can imagine how much rest Sammy would get. I don't know if they're feuding these days, but you know perfectly well that, at minimum, Frank would send over a purebred Afghan. Even if they were feuding.

I think what we would probably do is lay low and order a lot of Chinese food. I have a hunch that Sammy can eat Chinese takeout food every night of the week. I know I can, and the Chinese takeout delivery guys are very discreet. So we would stay at my place. I'd give him the sleeping loft, and I'd throw some sheets on the couch downstairs for me. I would do that for Sammy to pay him back for all the joy he's given me down through the years. And I would resist the temptation to ask him to sing, even though I would flip out if he so much as started humming. Can you imagine him humming "The Candy Man"? *In my apartment?* Let's not even discuss it.

Another reason I would give him the sleeping loft is that there is no phone up there. I would try like the devil to keep him away from the phone, because I know the second he saw one he would start thinking about his commitments, and it would be impossible for the guy not to make at least one call to the Coast. So I'd just try to keep him comfortable for as long as possible, although pretty soon my friends would begin wondering what ever happened to me, and it would take all the willpower in the world not to let on that I had Sammy Davis in my loft and was giving him a complete rest.

I don't kid myself that I could keep Sammy Davis happy in my loft for a full couple of months. He would be lying on the bed, his frail muscular body looking lost in a pair of boxer shorts, and before long I would hear those fingers snapping, and I would know that the wiry little great entertainer was feeling penned up and it would be inhuman to expect him to stay there any longer. I think that when I sensed that Sammy was straining at the leash, I would rent a car—a Ford LTD (that would be a switch for him, riding in a Middle American car)—and we would ride out to my sister and brother-in-law's place in Jersey. He would probably huddle down in the seat, but somehow I have the feeling that people in passing cars would spot him. We'd be lucky if they didn't crash into telephone poles. And if I know Sammy, whenever someone recognized him he wouldn't be able to resist taking off his shades and graciously blowing them a kiss.

The reason I would take Sammy to my sister and brother-in-law's house is because they're simple people and would not hassle him—especially my brother-in-law. My sister would stand there with her hands on her hips, and when she saw me get out of the Ford with Sammy, she would cluck her tongue and say, "There goes my crazy brother again," but she would appear calm on the surface, even though she would be fainting dead away on the inside. She would say something like "Oh, my God, I didn't even clean the floors," but then Sammy would give her a big hug and a kiss, and I'm sure that he would make a call, and a few weeks later she would have a complete new dining-room set, the baby grand she always wanted and a puppy.

She would put Sammy up in her son's room (he's away at graduate school), saying she wished she had something better, but he would say, "Honey, this is just perfect." And he would mean it, too, in a way, my nephew's bedroom being an interesting change from those one-thousand-dollar-a-day suites at the Tropicana. My brother-in-law has a nice easygoing style and would be relaxing company for Sammy, except that Al does work in television and there would be a temptation on his part to talk about the time he did the "Don Rickles Show" and how different and sweet a guy Don is when you get him offstage. If I know Sammy, he would place a call to CBS—with no urging from any of us—and see to it that Al got to work on his next special. If the network couldn't do a little thing like that for him, the hell with them, he would get himself another network. Sammy's that kind of guy.

One danger is that my sister, by this time, would be going out of her mind and wouldn't be able to resist asking Sammy if she could have a few neighbors over on a Saturday night. Let's face it, it would be the thrill of a lifetime for her. I would intercede right there, because it wouldn't be fair to the guy, but if I know Sammy he would tell her, "Honey, you go right ahead." She would have a mixed group over—Italians, an Irish couple, some Jews, about twelve people tops—and she would wind up having the evening catered, which of course would lead to a commotion when she tried to pay for the stuff. No way Sammy would let her do that. He would buy out the whole delicatessen, give the delivery guy a C note and probably throw in an autographed glossy without being asked.

Everyone at the party would pretend to be casual, as if Sammy Davis weren't there, but before long the Irish space salesman's wife (my sister's crazy friend, and what a flirt *she* is) would somehow manage to ask him to sing, and imagine Sammy saying no in a situation like that. Everyone would say just one song, but that bighearted son of a gun would wind up doing his entire repertoire, probably putting out every bit as much as he does when he opens at the Sands. He would do it all—"The Candy Man," "What

Kind of Fool Am I," tap-dance, play the drums with chop-
sticks on an end table, do some riffs on my nephew's old
trumpet and work himself into exhaustion. The sweat would
be pouring out of him, and he would top the whole thing
off with "This Is My Life" ("and I don't give a damn"). Of
course, his agents on the Coast would pass out cold if they
ever got wind of the way he was putting out for twelve
nobodies in Jersey. But as for Sammy, he never did know
anything about halfway measures. He either works or he
doesn't, and he would use every ounce of energy in that
courageous little show-biz body of his to see to it that my
sister's friends—that mixed group of Italians, Irish and
Jews—had a night they'd never forget as long as they lived.

Of course, that would blow the two months of complete
rest, and I would have to get him out of Jersey fast. By
that time, frankly, I would be running out of options. Once
in a while, I pop down to Puerto Rico for a three- or four-
day holiday, but, let's face it, if I showed up in San Juan
with Sammy, first thing you know, we would be hounded
by broads, catching the show at the Flamboyan, and Dick
Shawn would be asking Sammy to hop up onstage and do
a medley from *Mr. Wonderful*. (He was really something
in that show, battling Jack Carter tooth and nail, but too
gracious to use his bigger name to advantage.)
Another possibility would be to take Sammy out to see
a professor friend of mine who teaches modern lit at San
Francisco State and would be only too happy to take us in.
That would represent a complete change for Sammy, a
college campus, but as soon as the school got wind he was
around, I'll bet you ten to one they would ask him to speak
either to a film class or the drama department or even a
political-science group. And he would wind up shocking
them with his expertise on the Founding Fathers and the
philosophy behind the Bill of Rights. The guy reads, and

I'm not talking about *The Bette Davis Story*. Anyone who sells Sammy Davis short as an intellectual is taking his life in his hands.

In the end, Sammy and I would probably end up in Vermont, where a financial-consultant friend of mine has a cabin that he never uses. He always says to me, "It's there, for God's sake—use it." So I would take Sammy up there, away from it all, but I wouldn't tell the financial consultant who I was taking, because the second he heard it was Sammy Davis he would want to come along. Sammy and I would start out by going into town for a week's worth of supplies at the general store, and then we would hole up in the cabin. I'm not too good at mechanical things, but we would be sort of roughing it, and there wouldn't be much to do except chop some firewood, which I would take care of while Sammy was getting his complete rest.

I don't know how long we would last in Vermont. Frankly, I would worry after a while about being able to keep him entertained, even though he would be there for a complete rest. We could talk a little about Judaism, but, frankly, I would be skating on thin ice in that area, since I don't have the formal training he has or any real knowledge of theology. The Vermont woods would probably start us batting around theories about the mystery of existence, but to tell the truth, I'd be a little bit out of my depth in that department, too. He's had so much experience on panel shows, and I would just as soon not go one-on-one with him on that topic.

Let's not kid around, I would get tense after a while, and Sammy would feel it. He would be too good a guy to let on that he was bored, but pretty soon he would start snapping those fingers and batting out tunes on the back of an old Saturday Evening Post or something, and I think I would crack after a while and say, "Sammy, I tried my best to supply you with a couple of months of complete

rest, but I'm running out of gas." He would tap me on the
shoulder and say, "Don't worry about it, babe," and then,
so as not to hurt my feelings, he would say he wanted to
go into town to get some toothpaste. So he would drive in,
with the eye and all, and I know damned well the first
thing he would do is call his agents on the Coast and ask
them to read him the "N.Y. to L.A." column of a few
*Varietys*. Next thing you know, I would be driving him to
the airport, knowing in my heart that I hadn't really suc-
ceeded. He would tell me that any time I got to the Coast
or Vegas or the Springs, and I wanted anything, *anything*,
just make sure to give him a ring. And the following week,
I would receive a freezer and a videotape machine and a
puppy.

So I think I'm just not the man to get Sammy Davis the
complete rest he needs so desperately. However, I certainly
think someone should. How long can he keep driving that
tortured little frame of his, pouring every ounce of his
strength into the entertainment of Americans? I know, I
know—there's Cambodia and Watergate, and, believe me,
I haven't forgotten our own disadvantaged citizens. I know
all that. But when you think of all the joy that man has
spread through his night-club appearances, his albums, his
autobiography, his video specials and even his movies, which
did not gross too well but were a lot better than people
realized, and the things he's done not only for his friends
but for a lot of causes the public doesn't know about—
when you think of all that courageous little entertainer has
given to this land of ours, and then you read that he's
trying, repeat *trying*, to get a few months off for a complete
rest and he can't, well, then, all I can say is that there's
something basically rotten in the system.

—1974.